SHARP AS A BLADE

The four hit men were closing in on Don Pucci's party.

Blade did the only thing he could—he suddenly crouched in front of the Don's wheelchair, aimed the Commando barrel over Pucci's right shoulder, and sighted on one of the trigger men with a pistol, the nearest one.

Blade cut loose, the Commando chattering loudly, the stock bucking against his shoulder.

The closest hit man took a burst in the chest and was flung to the carpet.

The hit man with the sawed-off shotgun let fly into the back of one of the Don's men at point-blank range, the buckshot blowing the man's chest out and sending him sprawling. Pivoting, the hit man took a bead on the Don.

Blade squeezed the trigger, stitching the shotgun-wielding killer from the crotch to the forehead.

Also in the *Endworld series:*

THE FOX RUN
THIEF RIVER FALLS RUN
TWIN CITIES RUN
KALISPELL RUN
DAKOTA RUN
CITADEL RUN
ARMAGEDDON RUN
DENVER RUN
CAPITAL RUN
NEW YORK RUN
LIBERTY RUN
HOUSTON RUN
ANAHEIM RUN
SEATTLE RUN

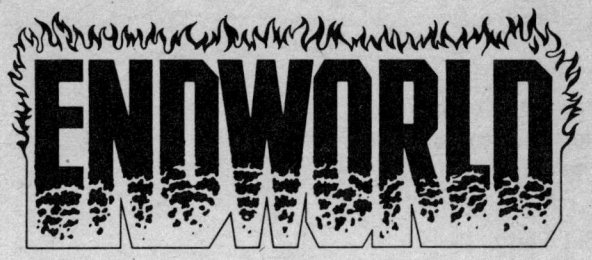

#15: NEVADA RUN
DAVID ROBBINS

LEISURE BOOKS   NEW YORK CITY

*Dedicated to
Judy and Joshua and Shane
Van and Amadon
Enoch and Elijah
and to the oldest profession of all . . .
the art of storytelling*

A LEISURE BOOK

April 1989

Published by

Dorchester Publishing Co., Inc.
276 Fifth Avenue
New York, NY 10001

Copyright © 1989 by David Robbins

All rights reserved. No part of this book may be reproduced or transmitted in any form or by any electronic or mechanical means, including photocopying, recording, or by any information storage and retrieval system, without the written permission of the Publisher, except where permitted by law.

The name "Leisure Books" and the stylized "LB" with design are trademarks of Dorchester Publishing Co., Inc.

Printed in the United States of America.

PROLOGUE

Should he waste the scuzz now or later? Johnny Giorgio glanced over his right shoulder at the source of his irritation and frowned. His diamond-shaped face, with its hard, cruel features, became even more severe. A flinty narrowing of his brown eyes accompanied a bunching of his bushy black eyebrows. He lifted his left arm and swiped at the bangs of his oily black hair.

"I still say this is the craziest damn idea you ever came up with," Manzo complained for the umpteenth time. His rodentlike countenance twitched as he spoke, his dark eyes flicking over the landscape on both sides of Highway 59. His dark brown suit, unlike Giorgio's neat, black three-piece, was rumpled and in need of a washing.

Giorgio pursed his lips thoughtfully, his right hand resting on the machine gun in his lap, a Weaver Arms Nighthawk. He was tempted to order his driver to stop the jeep so he could show Manzo what happened to underlings who chronically complained, but he refrained for two reasons. First, he might need Manzo when he made the snatch. Secondly, he estimated they were within ten miles of their destination, and he didn't want anyone from the Home to hear the gunfire.

No.

He would bide his time.

Play it real smart.

And rack the son of a bitch the first chance he got!

The two green jeeps, decades ago the property of the Nevada National Guard, continued northward on 59. A new road sign appeared on the right: HALMA. FOUR MILES.

Giorgio gazed at the road sign in perplexity. What the hell was this? Was Halma inhabited? His snitch had never said nothing about Halma.

Manzo, seated in the rear of the jeep directly behind Giorgio, spotted the sign. "Look at that!"

"I see it," Giorgio said calmly.

"You know what that means?" Manzo asked belligerently.

Giorgio twisted in his seat and stared at the two men in the back, Manzo and the other trigger man, Ianozzi, who was sitting behind the driver. He focused his full attention on Manzo, composing himself so his anger was carefully concealed. "I know what it means," he said in a quiet tone.

Ianozzi, a young man of 25 wearing a blue suit and tie, gazed at Giorgio for a few seconds, then casually placed both of his hands on the Mossberg Model 500 Bullpup resting across his knees.

"Why did we have to come so far?" Manzo queried, nervously surveying the woods bordering the highway. He failed to note the expression on Giorgio's face. His fatigue and apprehension combined to make him careless. "Who cares what's in Minnesota?"

"I've explained it to you many times," Giorgio noted patiently.

Manzo scowled. "I just don't like being this far from Vegas. We could have done this another way."

"This is the best way," Giorgio assured him. "Trust me."

Manzo's weasely eyes shifted to Giorgio. "I trust you, Boss. You know that."

"Do I?" Giorgio said. "I'm beginning to wonder."

Manzo abruptly realized his mistake. He blanched and swallowed hard. "Hey, no offense meant, Boss! I was just letting off a little steam. We've been on the road for over a week, and all the muties and creeps can get to a guy. You know how it is."

"I know how it is," Giorgio said.

Manzo mustered a weak grin. "I'm a little antsy, is all. All this nature shit makes me uncomfortable. I'm used to the casinos, the broads, and the booze. Hell! I ain't been laid in over a week!"

"None of us have been laid since we left," Giorgio observed. "But you don't hear none of the other guys griping."

Manzo voiced a feeble titter. "Don't take it personal, Boss. I can't help it if I'm edgy."

"A wiseguy can't afford to get edgy," Giorgio noted. "You know the saying: If you blow your cool, you're a fool." He paused. "I don't like fools in my organization."

"It won't happen again," Manzo vowed. "I promise!"

Giorgio glanced at the other trigger man, Ianozzi. "Did you hear that, Ozzi? He says it won't happen again."

Ozzi's green eyes brightened, his thin lips curling upward. "I heard it, Boss."

The driver suddenly slammed on the brakes, causing the jeep to lurch slightly as it abruptly slowed.

Giorgio gripped the dash with his left hand for support. "What the hell are you doing, Sacks?" he demanded.

Sacks was gripping the black steering wheel tightly, his brown eyes on the highway ahead, his bulldog visage registering amazement. "Look! Up ahead!" He began to gradually accelerate.

Giorgio swiveled and faced front.

Highway 59 was awash with the bright May sunlight. Two hundred yards distant walked a quartet consisting of two men and two women, none of whom appeared to be much over 20 years old. One of the women was a blonde, the other a redhead. The blonde wore blue shorts and a faded yellow blouse; the redhead was wearing light brown pants and a green blouse. Both of the men wore jeans. One, the heftier of the pair, also wore a dark green T-shirt and carried a shotgun; the leaner of the men had on a brown shirt and was armed with a revolver in a holster on his right hip. All four were heading to the north, their backs to the approaching jeeps.

"Do we snuff 'em?" Manzo asked eagerly.

"No," Giorgio replied. "Chill out and let me do the talking."

Alerted by the roar of the jeep motors, the quartet had turned and were watching the vehicles draw ever nearer. The man with the shotgun hustled the others to the right side of the road, their expressions conveying their apprehension.

Giorgio gazed over his left shoulder and out the rear window, spying the second jeep 25 yards to the rear, the jeep containing three more of his best soldiers—Pete, Tommy, and Nicky—as well as most of their supplies, their food and water and spare gas.

"You want me to pull up next to them, then?" Sacks inquired.

Giorgio stared at his driver. Sacks was one of the old-time boys, and there were flecks of gray in his brown hair. Although Sacks was unquestionably loyal, his intellect was on a par with a turnip's. "No," Giorgio cracked, "I want you to run them over." He paused. "Of course I want you to pull up next to them! How else am I going to talk to them?"

Sacks flinched and angled the jeep to the right side of the road.

"Keep your hardware out of sight," Giorgio instructed his men. He slid the Nighthawk to the floor, then placed his right hand on the door latch. The doors on the jeeps were canvas affairs with thin plastic windows instead of glass, and the windows did not roll down. He waited until the jeep stopped approximately five yards from the quartet before opening the door and stepping out, smiling broadly.

"Hello," he greeted them.

The young men eyed him warily, the hefty one fingering the trigger of his shotgun, the lean one with his right hand on his revolver. Behind the men, the two women were clearly uneasy.

"Hello," Giorgio said again. "I hope we didn't scare you."

The second jeep was coasting to a halt behind the first.

"Who are you?" the hefty youth queried anxiously. "What do you want?"

Giorgio deliberately maintained his friendly facade. He took a step away from the door, his hands at his sides to show he was unarmed and ostensibly not a threat. "Sorry to bother you, but we're lost."

"Lost?" the hefty youth repeated skeptically.

"Yes," Giorgio lied. "We're looking for a place called the Home. Have you ever heard of it?"

The redheaded woman grinned in relief. "I'm from the Home. Who are you?"

"You're from the Home!" Giorgio stated in delight. "I can't believe my luck! We've traveled so far to get here, all the way from Nevada."

"Are the Elders expecting you?" the redhead asked.

"I don't know who the Elders are," Giorgio admitted.

"The Elders are responsible for managing the Home," the redhead disclosed. "One of them, Plato, is our Leader."

The hefty youth's brown eyes narrowed. "You came all the way from Nevada to see the Family and you don't know about the Elders?"

Giorgio resisted an impulse to smash Hefty in the chops. "I was told a little about the Family. I know they live in a thirty-acre compound on the outskirts of what was once Lake Bronson State Park. And I heard a lot about the Warriors, the ones who defend the Home and protect the Family. But I wasn't told about the Elders." He didn't add that his only interest was in the Warriors; he couldn't care less about the damn Elders.

"The Spirit is smiling on you," the redhead said. "Blade

is at the Home right now. He's the head Warrior."

Giorgio nodded. "So I heard. The Warriors have quite a reputation."

Hefty grinned. "The Warriors are the best fighters in the world! Nobody's been able to beat them—not the Trolls, the Doktor, the Technics, the Russians, nobody," he said proudly.

"Are you from the Home too?" Giorgio questioned.

"No," Hefty replied. "I live in Halma, about three miles or so to the north. My people are called the Clan. We used to live in the Twin Cities, but the Warriors saved us from the Watchers and helped us to relocate in Halma. We wanted to live close to the Family."

"I'm the only one here from the Home," the redhead chimed in.

"How nice," Giorgio said politely. "How far is it to the Home from here?"

"Three miles to Halma," the hefty youth calculated aloud, "and then another mile to the cutoff. You take a right when you come to a dirt road. It runs about five miles, right up to the Home. You can't miss it."

Giorgio grinned. The Home was nine or ten miles away, which meant no one there would be able to hear the shots and none of the Warriors could reach the scene before he was long gone. Halma was much closer, but it didn't matter if any of the Clan heard the gunfire. "This is great news," he said.

"My name is Mindy," the redhead offered. "My mother is a Warrior."

Giorgio did a double take. "She is?"

"Yes," Mindy stated.

"Why didn't you say so before?" Giorgio queried.

Hefty chuckled. "Mindy's too modest. Her mom isn't as famous as Blade, Hickok, Yama, and the others, but she's one mean momma."

"Ted!" Mindy exclaimed in protest. "Don't talk about my mom that way!"

"Well, she is," Ted insisted.

"What is your mother's name?" Giorgio asked Mindy.

"Helen," she answered.

Giorgio could scarcely suppress his excitement. Here was exactly who he needed, delivered on a golden platter! "I look forward to meeting your mother. Would you consent to drive with us to the Home?"

"I don't know...." Mindy said, her blue eyes scrutinizing the jeeps.

"Come on," Giorgio urged her. "I would take it as a personal favor."

"I'd like to," Mindy said, "but I can't. Please don't be insulted, but we're taught to be very leery of strangers."

"Yeah," Ted concurred. "You haven't even told us your name yet."

"Anthony Pucci," Giorgio stated, accenting each syllable distinctly. He didn't want the kid to make a mistake. "But you can call me Tony."

"I'm sorry I can't go with you, Tony," Mindy said.

"That's perfectly okay," Giorgio assured her. "It's understandable in this day and age. You can't be too trusting."

"Why do you want to see the Family?" Ted inquired.

"That's my business," Giorgio replied, a touch testily. The shit-head was too nosy for his own good!

"Just ask for Blade or Plato when you reach the Home," Mindy advised. "The Family is always happy to see strangers if they come in peace."

Giorgio turned toward the jeep. "I'll do that. And I thank you for your time."

Ted peered into the first jeep. "Who are those guys?" he asked.

"Associates of mine," Giorgio said. He moved up to the jeep, standing with the door between the quartet and him, staring at them through the plastic window. "Say, do you like chocolate candy?"

"I've never tasted it," Ted rejoined.

Giorgio grinned. Now it was his turn to razz the shit-head. "You've never had chocolate candy?"

"No," Ted responded.

"Don't you eat sweets?" Giorgio queried.

"Sweets aren't good for the body," Mindy interjected. "The Elders teach all of the Family children about sweets. We know there was a public mania for sugar-based foods before the Big Blast. The American people downed tons of sweets each day. Many of them were addicted, which is sad when you think about it, because excessive sugar consumption disrupts our metabolism."

Giorgio shrugged. "Some candy now and then never hurt nobody." He looked at Hefty. "What about you? You're from the Clan, not the Family. Or do the Elders control the Clan too?"

"The Elders don't control anyone," Ted said stiffly. "They guide the Family and serve as teachers. We respect the Elders a lot." He paused. "As far as candy goes, where would we get it? I spent my childhood in the Twin Cities, where we had to fight for every scrap of food. There wasn't any candy to be found. Since we came to Halma, though, the Family members have taught us how to grow our own crops and to gather food from the forest. We use a lot of honey, and my mom can whip up some terrific honey treats. But we don't have any chocolate candy."

"That's too bad," Giorgio said. "You don't know what you're missing. I happen to have a box in the jeep. Would you like to taste some?"

The four exchanged glances.

"Sure," Ted declared for all of them. "Why not?"

Giorgio smiled and leaned into the jeep, bending forward and taking hold of the Weaver Arms Nighthawk. He slowly backed up, keeping the machine gun out of sight until the last possible second.

Ted had relaxed his grip on the shotgun and was saying something to Mindy. The lean youth had taken his hand from his revolver.

"If you think sweets are bad for the body," Giorgio commented casually, "wait until you see what lead does." He pivoted and leveled the Nighthawk.

The blonde screamed.

Giorgio smiled as he squeezed the trigger, shooting the first burst low and taking Ted off at the knees. The

Weaver's heavy slugs ripped into Ted's kneecaps, blowing them apart, tumbling Ted backwards and causing the shotgun to fall from his fingers.

The lean youth was clawing at his revolver.

Giorgio blasted the youth from the crotch to the chin, stitching a straight line of miniature red geysers, the impact flinging the lean one onto his back.

The blonde was still screaming, but not for long.

Sadistically, Giorgio let her have a few rounds in the face and she dropped with a strangled cry.

Mindy was gaping at Giorgio in horror, shocked to her core.

"The girl!" Giorgio snapped, and Ozzi, Sacks, and Manzo promptly emerged from the jeep. Ozzi and Sacks took hold of Mindy and started to propel her toward the vehicle.

"No!" Mindy shrieked, striving to wrench her arms free from their steely grasps.

Ozzi, holding his Bullwhip in his right hand and Mindy's right elbow in his left, unexpectedly rammed the Bullwhip barrel into her abdomen, doubling her over. "Move your ass, bitch!" he snarled.

"Don't damage the merchandise," Giorgio cautioned.

Ozzi and Sacks carted Mindy to the far side of the jeep and forced her to sit on the back seat.

Ted was on his left side, bent forward, clutching his legs above his ruined knees, whining and groaning, his eyes shut tight, in misery.

Giorgio walked up to the youth. "Open your eyes, punk!"

Ted's eyes didn't open. He trembled, breathing deeply.

Scowling, Giorgio hauled off and kicked the youth in the ribs.

Ted involuntarily cried out, tucking his right elbow against his side, his anguished brown eyes opening wide.

"That's better," Giorgio growled. He leaned down. "Listen up, punk, because I don't want you to forget any of this. Are you listening?"

Ted nodded vigorously.

"Good," Giorgio smirked. "When you see the Warriors, you tell them Anthony Pucci sends his regards. You got that?"

Tears rimming his eyes, Ted nodded.

"And I want you to give Blade a message," Giorgio directed. "I want you tell Blade we'll be waiting for him and the other Warriors. If Mindy's mom, Helen, wants to see her daughter again, then the Warriors must come to Las Vegas. They have one month. That's all. Just one month. If they don't show up by then, we whack the girl. Got that?"

Ted gulped and nodded.

"Tell Blade the girl will be waiting for them at the Golden Crown Casino. Remember that name. The Golden Crown Casino. Think you can remember that?"

Ted nodded yet again, then uttered a single word, his voice strained, his features in torment. "Why?"

Giorgio straightened. "Wouldn't you like to know," he said, and kicked the youth on the chin.

Ted's head snapped back, his teeth crunching together, and he went limp.

Someone snickered to Giorgio's rear.

"That's showing him, Boss!" Manzo said excitedly.

Giorgio turned.

Manzo stood three feet away, a Springfield Armory M1A rifle held loosely along his right side, idly gazing at the blood spurting from Ted's reputured kneecaps.

"Thanks for reminding me," Giorgio said.

Manzo looked up. "About what?"

"This," Giorgio stated, and shot Manzo in the stomach. He kept firing until all 25 rounds in the clip were expended, even after Manzo was down, and he grinned as he watched Manzo's body flopping and convulsing as it was hit again and again and again.

Ozzi was laughing.

"A good button man should be seen and not heard," Giorgio said, addressing the corpse contemptuously, then stalked to the jeep. "Let's hit the road," he announced. "We have a long ride ahead of us."

"What about Manzo's piece?" Ozzi asked.

"Leave it," Giorgio barked. "We don't need it." He slid into the jeep and glanced back at Mindy. "My plan worked like a charm."

Sacks took his seat behind the wheel. "I never doubted you for a minute, Boss," he said.

Giorgio ran his eyes up and down Mindy's attractive figure, then snickered. "Yes, sir! The trip back to Vegas is going to be a hell of a lot more interesting than the one coming out. Too bad Manzo won't be around to get a piece of the action." He cackled at his joke.

CHAPTER ONE

The giant stood on the rampart above the drawbridge situated in the center of the west wall of the Home and surveyed the cleared field beyond. His massive arms were folded across his huge chest, his muscles, even at rest, bulging in stark relief. He was wearing a black leather vest, green fatigue pants, and black combat boots. Around his waist was strapped a matched set of Bowies, one big knife on each hip. A comma of dark hair dangled over his brooding gray eyes.

He was worried.

What was he supposed to do?

The strain of living a dual life was beginning to take its toll, not on him but his marriage. His wife was miserable, and he couldn't bear to see her upset. Jenny and his son Gabe mattered more to him than anyone else in the world. He wanted to see them both happy, but Jenny could never be content with the status quo. And he couldn't blame her for her attitude because he was the reason for it. Or rather, his job was.

His two jobs.

He hadn't foreseen how difficult the task would be to juggle two positions at the same time. On the one hand, he was the head of the Warriors, pledged to safeguard the Family from any and all threats. And on the other hand, he was in charge of the Freedom Force, the elite tactical squad based in California. The Force, as it was known, had been the brainchild of the leaders of the Freedom Federation, the league of seven widespread factions devoted to preserving the fragments of civilization, to establishing order after 105 years of relative chaos. All thanks to the holocaust of World War Three.

Initially, he had moved Jenny and Gabe to California, to Los Angeles. But Jenny hated the city life. After so many years of togetherness and tranquility at the Home, she found the hustle and bustle of one of the few remaining major metropolises to be a constant source of anxiety. She also didn't like the fact he was seldom home, which essentially left her alone in a vast city of strangers.

The way he saw his problem, there were several choices. He could quit the Force or stop being the top Warrior, allowing him to spend more precious time with his wife and son. Or he could convince Jenny to return to the Home and continue his monthly trip to the compound, flying from LA to Minnesota on board one of the two VTOLs California possessed. The remarkable jets, with their vertical-take-off-and-landing capability, were utilized as a regular shuttle and courier service between the various Federation Factions. The aircraft were a godsend. What with the Family, the Clan, and the Moles in northern Minnesota, the Flathead Indians in Montana, the Cavalry in the Dakota Territory, the Civilized Zone in the Midwest, and the former state of California all comprising the Freedom Federation, they needed a means of traversing great distances rapidly and safely. Traveling overland between the factions was extremely dangerous; the barbaric Outlands were populated by savage bands of men and mutants.

So what should he . . .

There was a commotion on the rampart to his right, and

he twisted to find another Warrior jogging toward him. The newcomer was a lanky man dressed in buckskins, with long blond hair and a sweeping blond moustache, keen blue eyes, and a pair of pearl-handled Colt Python revolvers snug in their respective holsters.

"Hey, pard!" the gunman called out.

"What is it?" the giant asked, lowering his arms.

"Take a gander, Blade," the gunman directed, pointing to the west. "What do you reckon that's all about?"

Blade gazed westward. The Family diligently kept the fields surrounding their walled compound stripped of all vegetation for 150 yards to discourage any hostile attack. The 20-foot-high brick walls topped with sharp barbed wire afforded an excellent view of all approaches. No one could cross the fields without being seen. Just past the fields the dense forest began, unbroken for miles and miles except for the crude dirt road the Family and the Clan had constructed running from the Home to Highway 59.

And there on the road, barreling toward the Home at a reckless speed, stirring up a cloud of dust in the process, was an old flatbed truck.

Blade's eyes narrowed. He recognized that truck. The Clan had received the vehicle in trade with the Civilized Zone. All seven Federation factions now engaged in periodic trade and barter sessions. The Family often traded vegetables, venison jerky, buckskin clothing sewn together by the Weavers, and other items for commodities the other factions owned in abundance.

"That hombre is going like a bat out of hell," the gunfighter commented in his typical Western idiom.

"This could be trouble," Blade mentioned.

"Do you want me to sound the alarm?" the gunman asked.

Blade reflected for a moment. Why should he arouse the Family and interrupt whatever the rest of the Warriors were doing without justification? The Warriors in Beta Triad were probably still sleeping; Rikki, Yama, and Teucer had been on wall duty during the night, and it was only midmorning. "No, Hickok," Blade said. "We won't get everybody all excited until we know what's going on."

"Makes sense to me, pard," Hickok declared.

The truck was several hundred yards off, swerving and bouncing as the driver hit a series of bumps and ruts.

"We really should have made that road a mite smoother," Hickok observed. "It's murder on the kidneys."

"We did the best we could considering we don't have any heavy construction equipment," Blade remarked. He leaned out over the edge of the rampart, careful not to entangle himself in the barbed wire, and insured the drawbridge was down so the truck could enter. The drawbridge opened outward from the brick wall, permitting access to the Home over the inner moat. The Founder of the Home, a man named Kurt Carpenter, had diverted a stream into the northwest corner of the compound and channeled the water along the inner base of all four walls, then out the southeast corner. The moat was yet another of the defenses the Founder had incorporated into the design of his survivalist retreat immediately prior to the war.

"Should we mosey down and see what the fuss is all about?" Hickok inquired.

"Let's," Blade said.

"What about Geronimo?" Hickok questioned.

Blade hesitated. Together, Hickok, Geronimo, and himself composed Alpha Triad. The Warriors were divided into triads to increase their efficiency; the three Warriors in each of the six triads became the closest of friends and functioned as supremely deadly, tight-knit teams. He knew Geronimo was patrolling the ramparts, and was most likely somewhere on the east wall. Since the walls enclosed an area 30 acres in size. Geronimo would not return for another ten minutes. "If we need him, I'll send for him," Blade said, and hurried to the stairs leading from the rampart to the inner bank of the moat. He descended quickly and crossed to the bridge, the gunman at his side.

"I just hope the cow chip doesn't run over somebody," Hickok commented.

Nearby, the Family members were busily involved in

their everyday activities. While the eastern half of the compound was preserved in a natural state for agricultural purposes, the western half contained the enormous concrete blocks the Founder had built to withstand the devastation of the war, and was where the Family generally congregated and socialized.

The flatbed was now less than a hundred yards away and closing.

"We'll meet him outside," Blade said, and hastened across the drawbridge to the field.

"How do we know it's a guy?" Hickok noted. "It could be a gal."

"Could be," Blade agreed.

Whoever was driving was pushing the vehicle to its limits. The engine was roaring and belching puffs of smoke out the exhaust.

"Maybe we should put up a Stop sign at the edge of the trees," Hickok quipped. "We don't want hot-rodders tearing up the Home."

Blade glanced at the gunfighter. "Where did you learn about hot-rodders?"

"In the library. Where else?" Hickok responded.

Kurt Carpenter had stocked one of the concrete blocks with hundreds of thousands of books. He had realized his descendants would require knowledge if they were to persevere after World War Three, and he had filled his library with volumes on every conceivable subject. The Family members prized the books as their primary means of education and as a source of entertainment. The photographic books depicting life before the Big Blast, as they referred to the war, were especially valued. Blade pondered all of this as he watched the flatbed come to a screeching stop not 15 feet away. "Let's go," he said, running up to the driver's door.

The window was down, revealing the features of the leader of the Clan. Zahner was his name, and he had fine brown hair parted on the left, blue eyes, a cleft in the middle of his upper lip, and a square jaw. He took one look at the Warriors and motioned for them to climb in.

"Hurry!" he goaded them.

"Not so fast," Blade stated. "Is the Clan under attack?"

"No," Zahner said. "But two of my people are dead and Mindy is missing. We think she's been kidnapped."

"Mindy? Kidnapped?" Blade said in disbelief. He started around the cab. "Hickock!" he ordered. "Now you can sound the alarm. Assemble all of the Warriors and man all of the walls. Don't let anyone out of the compound until you hear from me. And run a check to see if anyone besides Mindy is missing."

"Will do, pard," Hickok promised. "What do I tell Helen?"

Blade, about to open the passenger door, paused, his lips compressing. "Don't say a word to her yet. Not until we find out what's happened."

Hickok nodded his understanding, wheeled, and sprinted into the Home.

Blade climbed up into the cab and slammed the door.

"Hang on," Zahner advised, tramping on the gas and executing a tight U-turn. The flatbed raced toward Highway 59.

"Fill me in," Blade instructed the Clan leader.

"The details are still sketchy," Zahner said, bouncing on the seat as the truck struck a rut. "You'll need to talk to Ted." He frowned. "If he can talk."

"Ted? Isn't he the one Mindy's been seeing?" Blade inquired. "Helen mentioned they are getting quite serious about their intentions."

"Ted's the one," Zahner confirmed. He was wearing faded, patched jeans and a blue shirt.

"Tell me what you know," Blade reiterated.

"I was at home with Becky about an hour ago when a runner showed up at my door," Zahner detailed, keeping his eyes on the road. "As you know, not all of the Clan live within the Halma town limits. A lot of my people live outside of Halma. They've built their own homes or taken over abandoned property. Anyway, a family living south of town apparently heard some gunfire this morning.

Automatic gunfire." He swerved to avoid a bump.

"Go on," Blade said.

"The husband and his oldest son went to investigate," Zahner continued. "They found Ted barely alive and another couple, Faron and Grace, dead."

"What about Mindy?"

"Ted's parents told me Mindy had dropped by early this morning," Zahner replied. "Evidently the two couples got together and decided to go for a stroll. You know how it is when you're young and in love. But to answer your question, no, there was no sign of Mindy."

"Were they armed?" Blade asked. None of the Family members were allowed to venture outside the Home unless they were armed or escorted by a Warrior.

Zahner nodded. "Yep. Ted and Faron weren't dummies. Ted took his dad's shotgun and Faron had a revolver. Fat lot of good it did them."

"Will Ted live?"

"I don't know," Zahner said. "We don't have Healers, like your Family does, but we do have some people skilled in the herbal arts. Ted is being treated right now. They took him to the building we're using as our town hall. I jumped in the truck and took off the first chance I got."

"I appreciate it," Blade stated. "The sooner we act, the better. Do we know who shot them yet?"

"No," Zahner said. "Ted wasn't able to talk before I left. I have search parties out looking for Mindy and their attackers."

"What makes you think Mindy was kidnapped?" Blade queried.

"Ted," Zahner said.

"But you just said you weren't able to talk to him," Blade noted.

"I wasn't," Zahner explained. "But he was mumbling a lot, almost in shock. He said something about Mindy being taken."

"If someone took Mindy," Blade vowed, "they'll pay. No one attacks the Family or any of our allies with impunity."

"I just hope Ted doesn't die before he can fill us in," Zahner mentioned.

They drove in silence for a while, the truck eating up the distance between the Home and Highway 59.

"I wonder if the Russians could be behind it," Zahner commented.

"I doubt it," Blade said. The Russians controlled a large section of what was once the eastern United States, and the Reds and the Family had clashed before. Each time the Russians had lost, and they were determined to eradicate the Family at all costs.

"Why?" Zahner wanted to know. "The Russians sent a commando squad here once before, remember? Specifically to kidnap one of your Family, as I recall."

"True," Blade conceded. "But they failed, and I can't see them trying the same scheme twice. When they strike back at us, they'll come up with a bigger and better idea. Besides, why would they take Mindy? She's, what, nineteen? She wouldn't be able to give them much information."

"The Russians wouldn't know that," Zahner said, disputing the Warrior. "But even if the Russians aren't responsible, it could be any of the other enemies we've made over the years."

"You've got a point there," Blade admitted.

"Whoever did this wanted someone from the Home," Zahner observed.

"You don't know that for sure," Blade said.

"Don't I? Why were only my people shot? If whoever attacked them wanted women, why was Grace killed? Are you trying to tell me it was just coincidence that the only one left alive was Mindy? That the only one apparently kidnapped was from your Family?" Zahner countered.

Blade stared at the Clan leader, musing. Zahner might have a point, and the implications were unsettling.

"I don't see how you do it," Zahner said.

"Do what?"

"Take all the pressure," Zahner said. "I mean, here you

are, the head of the Warriors, responsible for the lives of around a hundred people at the Home, and you go and take the added responsibility of leading the Freedom Force. I just don't see how you take on all the pressure. It's rough for me sometimes, knowing so many lives depend on my judgment."

"You have more people to look out for," Blade reminded the Clansman. "Don't you have about five hundred in the Clan?"

"Five hundred and three, to be exact," Zahner said.

"So it's a lot harder on you than it is on me," Blade stated.

"I don't care whether the number is one hundred or five hundred," Zahner said. "Being responsible for so many lives is a heavy burden. And since you're also the head of the Force, every Federation group is relying on you." He looked at the Warrior. "Don't you ever think about it? Doesn't it ever get to you?"

Blade felt like laughing but refrained. "I try not to dwell on the responsibility too much. I just take it a day at a time and do the best I can."

"All I know is I wouldn't want to be in your shoes," Zahner remarked.

The flatbed reached Highway 59 and Zahner jerked on the steering wheel, taking a left.

Blade gazed down at his combat boots. Maybe Zahner had another point. Truth was, sometimes *he* felt like he didn't want to be in his own shoes. Everyone undoubtedly felt the same way at one time or another. Learning to take the bad with the good was one of the major lessons every person had to experience.

But such was life.

CHAPTER TWO

The Clan was using a two-story brick structure as their meeting place. They had selected the building because it was centrally located in Halma and because most of the windows were still intact, a rarity in postwar structures.

Zahner brought the flatbed to an abrupt stop alongside the cracked curb and jumped out.

Blade was already out and bounding up the cement stairs to the doors. A crowd had gathered on the steps and along the walk, but they quickly parted to permit his passage. He pulled on the right-hand door and entered the cool interior. Over a dozen people lined both sides of the corridor.

Zahner came through the door behind the giant. He moved past the Warrior and headed for the second door on the right. "How is he?" he asked, addressing a portly man with a balding pate attired in green trousers and a black shirt.

The portly man frowned. "He's awake. You can talk to him, but don't stay in there long. He needs his rest."

Blade joined Zahner.

"This is Striber," the Clan leader said, introducing the

portly man. "He's the closest thing to a Healer we've got."

"I know who you are," Striber said to Blade. "Everyone knows who you are."

"What are Ted's chances?" Blade questioned.

"He'll live, if that's what you mean," Striber replied. "But he'll be on crutches for years, maybe for the rest of his life."

"Crutches?" Blade repeated quizzically.

Striber frowned. "Whoever the bastards were, they shot out his knees. Deliberately, I'd say. Ted is fortunate his legs won't need to be amputated below the knees. As it is, he may never walk again. We'll have to wait and see how he heals. You never know. With the proper rehabilitation and training he could, conceivably, regain very limited use of his legs."

"Why did you say they deliberately shot him in the knees?" Blade asked.

"Because of what they did to the other three," Striber said.

"Three?" Blade interrupted. "But Zahner said only Faron and Grace were killed?"

Striber glanced at the Clan leader. "Didn't you tell him about the stranger?"

Zahner raised his right hand and smacked his forehead. "Damn! I was so worried about Ted and Mindy, I forgot! We found another body with the rest, someone who isn't from the Clan."

"I'd like to take a look at this body after I talk to Ted," Blade stated.

"The stranger was shot to ribbons," Striber mentioned. "You'll see for yourself. A drastic case of overkill. And it was the same with Faron and Grace. But Ted was different. All they did to him was shoot him in the knees and kick him on the chin. A few of his teeth are broken, but they didn't break his jaw."

"Why did they spare Ted's life?" Blade queried.

"Ted can tell you that," Striber said, motioning toward the open door.

Blade moved to the doorway. Inside stood a couple with grayish brown hair and homespun clothing next to a couch on which was a pale, heavyset youth who was covered from his chin to his feet by a white sheet. The lower portion of his face was swollen and bruised. "Hello," Blade said, and entered.

Zahner came in behind the Warrior. "Blade, these are Dan and Agnes, Ted's parents."

Blade nodded grimly. "I'm sorry about your son."

Agnes sniffled and dabbed at her moist eyes with an old handkerchief, evidently her husband's, she was holding in her left hand.

"Why would anyone do this to my boy?" Dan asked angrily. "Ted has never hurt anyone."

"I don't know why they did it," Blade said. "But we'll find the parties responsible and they will pay for what they've done. It's small consolation, I know."

"Are you going after them?" Dan inquired.

"Yes," Blade said.

"Good! Kill the scum for me!" Dan declared.

"Dan!" Agnes exclaimed, aghast.

"Would you mind if I talked to your son in private?" Blade asked them.

Dan took his wife's elbow in his right hand. "We'll be right outside."

"I won't take long," Blade promised.

The parents silently departed, Agnes with tears streaming down her cheeks, Dan with his shoulders slumped in abject depression.

Blade squatted next to the youth. Ted's eyes were open but listless. Dried blood caked the corners of his mouth. "Ted? Can you hear me?"

Ted did not respond.

"Ted? This is Blade? I need to talk to you," Blade stated.

"Blade?" Ted said, rousing from his trauma-induced lethargy. He focused on the Warrior with an intent expression. "You're here!"

"I'm here," Blade said. He noticed the youth spoke

with great difficulty. "I'm sorry to impose at a time like this, but we must talk."

"It's all right," Ted asserted.

"I know you're in a lot of pain, but I must know what happened," Blade said, coaxing the youth.

Ted clicked his puffy lips. "Okay. Mindy, Faron, Grace, and I took a walk south of town. We were on our way back when two jeeps pulled up and a guy got out."

"Who was this guy?" Blade interjected. "Do you know?"

"He gave his name as Anthony Pucci," Ted revealed. "He was acting real nice and friendly, but I didn't like the looks of him. He claimed he needed directions to the Home. Said he'd come all the way from Nevada."

"Nevada!" Blade remarked in surprise.

"Yep," Ted went on. "He was polite at first, and he seemed very interested in Mindy after she told him her mom is a Warrior. He even offered us some candy. That's when . . ." Ted began, then stopped, torment etched in his features.

"Take it easy," Blade advised. "If you can't talk about it, I'll understand."

Ted inhaled deeply. "He shot us! For no reason at all, he shot us! He pretended to reach into his jeep for some candy, but he pulled a gun out instead. I was shot first and I didn't see the others get hit. I was in too much pain. But I dimly recall them forcing Mindy into the jeep."

"Did this Pucci say why they were taking her?" Blade questioned.

"No," Ted said sadly. "But he did tell me to give you a message."

Blade's forehead creased in bewilderment. "Me? He mentioned me by name?"

"He sure did," Ted stated. "I'll never forget his words! He wanted me to give the Warriors his regards. And he said to tell you that he'd be waiting for you and the other Warriors. He said if Helen wants to see Mindy again, then the Warriors must come to Las Vegas."

"Why Las Vegas?"

"I don't know," Ted answered. "He said if the Warriors don't show up in Las Vegas within one month, then Mindy will die."

"Was that all?" Blade asked.

"No," Ted replied. "There was one more thing. He said Mindy would be waiting for you at the Golden Crown Casino. He wanted me to be certain to remember the name. The Golden Crown Casino."

Blade was baffled. "And that was all? He didn't say anything else?"

"That was his message," Ted responded.

"Okay," Blade said. "What happened next?"

"That's when he kicked me," Ted said. "I don't remember anything else until I woke up on this couch."

Blade slowly straightened. "You said there were two jeeps. How many others were with Pucci?"

"I don't know," Ted said. "There were two or three in the first jeep, and I didn't see how many were in the second."

"What did Pucci look like?" Blade inquired.

"He was about six feet tall," Ted detailed. "His hair was black, his eyes brown. His face was kind of mean looking. I don't know how to describe it."

Blade placed his right hand on the youth's shoulder. "Why don't you get some rest? If I have any more questions I'll get back to you."

Ted's eyelids were beginning to droop. "I'll do whatever I can to help you out! We've got to save Mindy!"

"I know," Blade assured the youth. "Don't worry. We'll save her." He turned and walked into the corridor.

Dan and Agnes were waiting near the door.

"You can go on in," Blade directed them. "I'm through with Ted for now."

"Thank you," Dan responded.

Zahner stepped into the corridor and patiently waited for the parents to go into the room before he spoke. "So what did you make out of all that information?"

"I'm stumped," Blade confessed. "I don't know any Anthony Pucci. None of the Warriors have ever been to

Las Vegas, so far as I know. There doesn't seem to be any reason behind the attack."

"There has to be a reason," Zahner said. "Why else did they drive all the way here from Nevada?"

"I wish I knew," Blade stated. "Right now I'd like to see the body of the stranger."

"Follow me," Zahner said, and led the way down the corridor for another 30 feet until he stopped next to a closed door on the left. "The bodies are in here," he explained, then opened the door.

Blade strolled inside to find three long tables occupying the center of the room and a maple desk and a folding chair to his right. Each table was draped with a white sheet profiling the contours of a human figure underneath.

"This is the one with the stranger," Zahner said, moving to the table on the right. He lifted the sheet.

Blade walked to the head of the table and examined the corpse. The man's dark brown suit was soaked with blood. Someone had shot him repeatedly at point-blank range. "Why would they shoot one of their own men?" he wondered aloud.

"We found a rifle next to his body," Zahner disclosed. "It hadn't been fired."

"What do you make of his clothes?" Blade asked.

Zahner shrugged. "The suit looks new to me."

"It does," Blade agreed. "And we both know that the men in the Civilized Zone and California wear suits just like this one. It was the style the men were wearing before the war. Buckskins are the rule elsewhere, like in the Dakota Territory and in Montana. A lot of my Family wear buckskins too, because they're easy to make and they last a long time. Fabric like the material in this suit is hard to come by. Except for the Civilized Zone and California, there aren't any factories manufacturing this type of clothing. For that matter, there aren't many clothing manufacturers of any kind around, period. Which is why we must make buckskins or patch together old garments."

"Do you think there's a link between this Nevada

business and California or the Civilized Zone?" Zahner queried.

"Don't know," Blade said. "Maybe there's a manufacturing facility in Las Vegas." He paused. "What did you find in his pockets?"

"His pockets?" Zahner responded, sounding surprised.

Blade looked at the Clansman. "Yes. Didn't you go through his pockets?"

"No," Zahner said. "I had him brought here, along with the other bodies and Ted, and then took off for the Home. I didn't have time to search him."

"Then let's do it," Blade declared.

Zahner tugged on the sheet and it slid to the floor.

Blade quickly examined the man's pockets. He found a set of keys in the right front pants pocket and a wad of bills in the left. "Here," he said, handing both to Zahner. Next he inspected the jacket pockets. There was nothing in either of the outside ones, but he did discover two items in an inside left pocket. The first was a small black book, the second a circular piece of blue plastic with the words JOHNNY'S PALACE imprinted on both sides.

"There's two thousand dollars here," Zahner announced, having just counted the money.

Blade paged through the small black book. On each one was a list of names, and beside each name was an address and a seven digit number. Some of the names were businesses, like *Eddy's Garage*, and they were all arranged alphabetically. Acting on a hunch he turned to the Gs and there it was: *Golden Crown Casino. 6619 Las Vegas Boulevard. 273-1400.*

"What have you got there?" Zahner inquired.

"Something that will come in handy when we get to Las Vegas," Blade said, closing the book. "If we have to go that far."

"What do you mean?" Zahner asked.

"I want you to take me back to the Home right now," Blade directed. "Alpha Triad is going after the ones who took Mindy."

"You sure Plato will give the okay?"

"Of course," Blade said. "But even if he doesn't like the idea, there's nothing he can do about it. In times of crisis the Warriors are empowered to do whatever is necessary, and as the head Warrior I decide our course of action. Hickok, Geronimo, and I are going after these SOBs in the SEAL."

"Do you really think you can catch them?" Zahner questioned. "They've got a head start and there's no telling which route they'll take back to Las Vegas."

"I don't know if we can catch up with them before they reach Las Vegas," Blade stated. "But we've got to try for Mindy's sake. If need be, we'll go all the way to Vegas."

"I'd like to go along," Zahner proposed.

"No," Blade said flatly.

"Why not? If anyone has a right to go, it should be one of the Clan," Zahner insisted. "They killed two of us."

"I understand your feelings," Blade mentioned. "But Alpha Triad is accustomed to functioning as a team. We can't afford to be distracted by having to watch out for you or any other Clansman."

"I wouldn't get in your way," Zahner said.

"Sorry," Blade said, refusing to give in. "But the answer is no."

Zahner frowned. "Then do me a favor."

"Anything," Blade pledged.

"If you find whoever is responsible for killing Faron and Grace and shooting Ted," Zahner said angrily, "give them a taste of their own medicine."

"I'll make them regret the day they were born."

CHAPTER THREE

The SEAL had been the Founder's pride and joy. Kurt Carpenter had wisely anticipated the deterioration of civilization after World War Three. He knew society would fall apart at the seams; the government would collapse, social institutions would cease to exist, and the transportation system would crumble. Accordingly, Carpenter spent millions on a special vehicle, a prototype intended to serve his descendents in a world gone haywire. The Solar Energized Amphibious or Land Recreational Vehicle—or SEAL for short—was designed to navigate any terrain. Vanlike in build, the entire body was composed of a shatterproof and heat-resistant tinted green plastic. The floor was an impervious metal alloy. Four huge puncture-proof tires, each four feet high and two feet wide, supported the transport.

Carpenter had also incorporated armaments into the vehicle. Mercenaries had been hired at great expense. The weapons systems they had installed were activated by four toggle switches on the dash. A pair of 50-caliber machine guns were mounted in recessed compartments under each front headlight, and a miniaturized surface-to-air missile was fitted on the roof over the driver's seat. A rocket-launcher was hidden in the middle of the front grill, while a flame-thrower was situated in the center of the front fender surrounded by layers of insulation.

As its name implied, the SEAL was solar powered. The light was collected by two solar panels affixed to the roof, the energy was converted and stored in revolutionary batteries located in a lead-lined case under the vehicle. The scientists had proudly boasted the SEAL would continue to function for a thousand years provided the solar panels or the battery casings were not damaged.

All of these thoughts filtered through Blade's mind as he steered the SEAL southward along Highway 93 in northern Nevada. The highway was pitted with wide cracks and potholes, and many sections were buckled. But few were the obstacles the SEAL couldn't circumvent, and the past seven days of travel had been relatively uneventful.

A whole week on the road!

Blade was intensely disappointed they had been unable to overtake Mindy's abductors. He mentally reviewed the events of the week, speculating on what he could have done differently to achieve Mindy's rescue. Zahner had rushed him back to the Home, and he had informed the assembled Family about the tragedy. After a hasty meeting with Plato and the Elders, it had been unanimously agreed Alpha Triad should proceed after the culprits with all dispatch. The SEAL was always fully stocked and ready to go at a moment's notice. Alpha Triad, with one addition, had departed the Home within an hour of his return.

But they'd never been able to catch up to the jeeps.

Where had he gone wrong?

Blade had deduced the abductors would not dare to travel in a direct course from the Home to Las Vegas. Doing so would entail driving through the Dakota Territory, home of the Cavalry, and the Civilized Zone—both allies of the Family. The abductors would want to avoid all contact with Federation factions. Which meant the kidnappers either went due south from the

Home, hoping to bypass the Civilized Zone, and then swung to the west around Oklahoma or Texas, or else they traveled westward from Minnesota, skirting the Dakota Territory to the north, and then angled to the southwest through the northwest corner of Wyoming, avoiding the Mormons currently in control of Utah, and entering Nevada from the northeast. Blade had opted for the second route.

Acting on the theory the kidnappers would shun all large cities and towns, Blade had stuck to the secondary roads. At settlements along the way he had stopped and asked about the two jeeps. No one had seen them. Many of the inhabitants of the small towns and communities had fled at the sight of the SEAL or greeted the Warriors with unconcealed suspicion. But none of them, much to Blade's relief, had attacked his party. Twice the Warriors had seen bands of scavengers near the road, and three times they had passed mutants, but neither the scavengers or their bestial counterparts had shown any inclination to tackle the SEAL.

A voice intruded on the giant's reverie.

"How much longer before we reach Las Vegas, pard?" Hickok asked.

Blade glanced to his right. The transport was spaciously designed with two comfortable bucket seats in the front separated by a brown console. Behind the bucket seats was a single seat the width of the vehicle. The rear of the SEAL was a storage area piled high with provisions, their jerky and water and spare ammunition. In a compartment under the rear section were two spare tires and a toolbox. "I don't know how much longer," he replied. "Geronimo has the map. Ask him."

Hickok twisted in his seat and gazed at the man sitting behind him, one of the two best friends he had. "Hey, you mangy Injun! Wake up!"

Geronimo had been napping with his head resting against the window. He came instantly awake, his alert brown eyes surveying the highway ahead for any sign of trouble. Powerfully built, he was stocky with black hair and rugged features. He wore a green shirt, green pants, and moccasins. An Arminius .357 Magnum was in a shoulder holster under his right arm and a tomahawk was tucked under his deer hide belt. "What is it, O Great White Idiot?"

Blade, listening to their banter, smiled. Geronimo was rightfully proud of his Blackfoot heritage, and the Indian and the gunman constantly teased one another over their respective racial differences.

"Boy! You sure get nasty when someone interrupts your beauty sleep!" Hickok cracked.

"I'd rather wake up with my wife at my side instead of seeing your ugly puss," Geronimo observed.

"There's nothin' wrong with my face," Hickok retorted indignantly.

"Nothing a good head transplant wouldn't cure," Geronimo commented.

"Two points for Geronimo," Blade interjected, laughing, glad their light-hearted joking was alleviating the tension of the mission.

But not everyone riding in the SEAL agreed.

A harsh feminine voice intruded on their conversation. "If you morons are through clowning around, why don't we get down to business? How long before we reach Las Vegas?"

Blade looked into the rearview mirror at the speaker. She sat directly behind him, her luxurious amber hair cascading past her shoulders. Her eyes were a vivid green, her features exceptionally lovely. She wore a black leather vest similar to his, but hers was cut low in the front, displaying her ample cleavage. Tight black leather pants and boots covered her shapely legs. Around her slim waist were strapped a pair of Caspian 45-caliber automatics. And projecting above her left shoulder was the hilt of the 24-inch machete she invariably carried in a custom-designed sheath on her back, slanted between her shoulder blades. The sheath was held fast by a wide black strip of leather looped across her chest.

"Who are you callin' morons, lady?" Hickok demanded.

"If the shoe fits," Helen responded. "And don't call me lady. The name is Helen, and don't you forget it!"

"I know what your name is," Hickok snapped. "And I can understand your being upset about Mindy. But that doesn't give you call to go around insultin' people."

Helen bristled. "I'll insult you or any other *man* any time I damn well feel like it!"

"You keep it up and you'll be pickin' your teeth up from the floor," Hickok warned her. "The only ones who get to insult me on a regular basis are my missus and this crazy Injun. You've been belly-achin' ever since we left the Home. You never have a nice word for anyone. All you do is gripe. Did you treat your ex-husband like this?"

Helen's face became livid with fury. Her hands moved to her Caspians. "Why, you . . ."

"That's enough!" Blade barked, slamming on the brakes and bringing the SEAL to a grinding halt. He swiveled in his seat, glaring at Helen. "I don't ever want to see you threatening to pull your guns on a fellow Warrior again! You got that?"

"But—" Helen began.

"No buts about it!" Blade declared in annoyance. "Hickok's right! You've been a monumental pain in the butt this whole trip. I've tried to make allowances for your behavior. You've complained because you didn't think we were going fast enough, and you've complained because you didn't agree with the route I'm taking, and you've groused every time we made a rest stop. You rarely talk unless you're spoken to, and even then it's some smart-mouth reply." He paused. "I've given you the benefit of the doubt because of the turmoil you must be feeling over Mindy. But no more! I let you talk me into taking you along against my better judgment. Sure, Mindy's your daughter and you have a right to help rescue her. But you also have a wicked temper and a short fuse, not exactly ideal traits for a Warrior."

Helen seemed stung by the rebuke. "If you felt that way about me, why'd you ever accept me as a Warrior?"

"The decision wasn't up to me," Blade said. "You know the procedure for selecting a new Warrior. The candidate must be sponsored before the Elders by a Warrior of standing. Spartacus sponsored you. The Elders voted on whether to accept your candidacy or not, and they decided to appoint you as a Warrior."

"But you could have protested their decision," Helen noted. "They would have listened to you."

"I didn't think it was necessary," Blade informed her. "Your good qualities outweigh your bad. There isn't one Warrior who is perfect in every respect."

"Speak for yourself," Hickok quipped.

"To hear you talk, I didn't think I had any good qualities," Helen mentioned.

"You do," Blade assured her. "I've been following your progress ever since you were assigned to Omega Triad. You take orders well and you always do your best at whatever job you're given. You relate well with the other Warriors in your Triad. You're one of the best shots in the Family. And you believe in the ideals the Founder proclaimed. You have a lot of good qualities."

Helen visibly relaxed, her lips curling downward in self-reproach. "I'm sorry. I didn't realize I've been acting like a bitch. You were right. All I can think about is Mindy. She's all I have left in this world. If anything happens to her . . ." she said, and let the sentence trail off.

"We'll get Mindy back," Hickok told her. "Don't fret none."

"For those who might be interested," Geronimo spoke up, "I've calculated the distance to Las Vegas."

"Impossible," Hickok said. "You couldn't have."

"Why not?" Geronimo asked, puzzled.

"Because I didn't see you take off your moccasins," Hickok commented with a mischievous grin. "And I know we're more than ten miles away."

"Two points for Hickok," Blade said, accelerating.

For the first time since her daughter was kidnapped,

Helen mustered a smile.

Geronimo elected to ignore the barb. "We crossed what was once the state line not too long ago. We should be coming up soon on a small town called Contact. The map doesn't say how many people lived there before the war. It could be deserted like so many others we've seen."

"How far is it from Contact to Las Vegas?" Blade inquired.

"I estimate about four hundred and forty-six miles," Geronimo divulged. "Because of the terrible shape the highway is in, we've only been able to average forty miles an hour. At our present rate, it will take us eleven hours to reach Vegas." He consulted a watch on his left wrist. "It's ten in the morning now. So we could reach Vegas tonight if we drive straight through. It would mean driving after sunset, though."

Blade reflected for a minute. As a rule, he did not drive after dark. Spotting an ambush or other threat was next to impossible once the sun went down. He preferred to do most of his driving during the daylight hours.

"I vote we drive straight through," Hickok suggested. "The sooner we reach Las Vegas, the better. Besides, we haven't run into any trouble yet. Maybe our luck will hold until we reach Vegas."

"One thing I learned a long time ago," Blade mentioned, "is never to push your luck." He stared into the rearview mirror. "Helen, I know you probably won't agree with my decision, but I'm not going to push the SEAL to reach Vegas tonight. We don't want to waltz into a trap. They must be expecting us. So we'll take it nice and slow. Is that okay by you?"

"Whatever you say," Helen stated. "You're in charge."

"Hey! Look!" Geronimo exclaimed, leaning forward and pointing.

Blade's eyes narrowed as he saw the cluster of buildings approximately a quarter of a mile ahead.

A freshly painted billboard abruptly appeared on the right: MA'S DINER. STRAIGHT AHEAD. ALL YOU CAN EAT FOR $4.99.

"What the blazes!" Hickok declared.

"Who would open a diner in the middle of nowhere?" Geronimo asked.

"We haven't seen any other traffic since we left Wyoming," Helen remarked. "And that was a military patrol from the Civilized Zone."

"Maybe they get traffic here from time to time," Blade conjectured.

"Why don't we stop?" Hickok recommended. "I could use some home-cooked grub. Venison jerky gets a mite bland after a spell."

"I don't know . . ." Blade said doubtfully.

"Please, Blade," Helen urged. "If the kidnappers came this way, the people here might have seen them. They might know if Mindy is still alive." She paused. "Please."

Against his better judgment, Blade agreed. "Okay. We'll stop and eat our midday meal early, but I want everyone to stay on their toes."

"You're a worrywart, you know that?" Hickok declared. "This place is called Ma's Diner. What harm can a little old lady do to four Warriors, for cryin' out loud?" He snickered at the notion.

"For once I agree with Hickok," Geronimo said. "They wouldn't bother to advertise if they weren't serious about attracting customers."

"I hope you're right," Blade stated.

"Quit your worryin', pard," Hickok advised. "What could go wrong?"

CHAPTER FOUR

"Looks innocent enough to me," Hickok mentioned.

Blade kept his foot on the brake, still uncertain of the wisdom of stopping. The SEAL was idling on Highway 93 approximately 400 yards south of Contact. The town had appeared to be deserted, although several of the buildings had exhibited evidence of recent habitation; the doors and windows on three of the homes had been intact and clean, and one of the yards had sported a flower garden.

"What are we waitin' for?" Hickok queried impatiently.

Blade sighed. To their right was a gravel drive leading to a newly painted white structure. MA's DINER was painted in bold black letters on a wooden sign perched over the front entrance. Four vehicles were parked outside, prewar-model cars in surprisingly fine condition. "One of us must stay in the SEAL with the doors locked," he mentioned.

"I'll do it," Geronimo volunteered.

Blade took a right, slowly approaching the diner, thankful the SEAL's tinted plastic body enabled him to see out but prevented anyone from viewing the interior. If hostile eyes were peeking from the diner windows, they would be unable to ascertain how many were in the transport. He pulled into a parking spot between a vintage Ford on the left and a Chevy on the right, then turned off the engine.

"Are we takin' the long guns?" Hickok queried.

"Of course," Blade responded. "It doesn't pay to get too overconfident."

Hickok glanced at Geronimo. "How about passin' them up here, pard?"

Geronimo turned in his seat. On top of the pile of provisions in the rear section were four different firearms. One was a Navy Arms Henry Carbine in 44-40 caliber, Hickok's favorite rifle. Next to the Henry was Blade's machine gun, a Commando Arms Carbine, a fully automatic 45-caliber firearm with a 90-shot magazine. Also on the pile was Helen's weapon, an Armalite AR-180A Sporter Carbine. Geronimo handed each of the guns to the proper party, then took hold of his Browning BAR. All of the firearms the Warriors used came from the enormous armory the Founder had stocked in one of the concrete blocks at the Home.

"Keep the doors locked," Blade reiterated as he took hold of his door handle.

"I will," Geronimo promised. "What if you do run into trouble in there? If I hear gunfire, should I come on the run?"

"You don't budge from the SEAL no matter what," Blade directed. "The transport might be virtually impervious, but I'm not taking any chances. You stay here and guard the SEAL."

"Okay," Geronimo said reluctantly. "If I see anything suspicious while you're inside, I'll sound the horn."

"Good idea," Blade stated. He looked at Hickok and Helen. "Are you two ready?"

"I was born ready," Hickok declared.

Helen simply nodded.

Blade opened the door. "I'm leaving the keys in the ignition," he informed Geronimo. "If something does happen to us, you can drive off."

"I'm not going anywhere without you," Geronimo said.

Blade jumped out, waited for Helen to join him, then slammed the door.

Hickok closed his door and ambled around the front of the SEAL. "Do you smell what I smell?" he asked them.

The mouth-watering aroma of cooking food filled the dusty air.

"Smells like steak," Helen commented.

"We'd best be on our guard," Hickok said sarcastically. "These hombres could be fryin' a steak just to trick us, to lure us into their trap!" He chuckled.

"Keep it up," Blade admonished, and led the way up to the front entrance.

"I hear music," Helen said.

Blade heard it too. A man singing in a wailing, heart-wrenching style. He caught a few of the lyrics.

". . . your cheatin' heart . . ."

Blade grabbed the doorknob and pulled the brown wooden door wide open, then swiftly stepped inside, to the right of the doorway, flattening his broad back against the wall and leveling the Commando.

"Howdy, stranger!" a woman called out. "Welcome to Ma's!"

Blade surveyed the diner. On the opposite side of the room was a counter running the length of the one-story building. Behind the yellow counter were two people, an elderly matron with gray hair, horn-rimmed glasses, and a jowly jaw, and a tall man with black hair and a toothpick in his mouth. Both of them wore white clothes, including an apron. There were ten tables in the diner. At a table to the right sat three men dressed in ragged jeans and flannel shirts, cups of coffee before them. And at another table to the left of the door was a short, obese man in a grimy blue suit and a woman with bright red lipstick coating her thick lips and too much rouge on her cheeks. She was wearing a red dress.

None of them appeared to be armed.

"Howdy!" the matron repeated. "Come on in! Ain't no

one here going to bite you!" She smiled in a friendly, sincere fashion.

Hickok walked through the door as if he didn't have a care in the world. He took a look around and grinned. "Yep. Definitely a trap."

"You won't need that hardware, son," the matron said, nodding at Blade's Commando. "Our muffins don't usually fight back."

Hickok laughed.

Blade slowly lowered the Commando and advanced toward the counter. The men on the right and the couple on the left watched him for a moment, then suddenly shifted their attention to the doorway. Blade looked back.

Helen had just entered the diner, her Carbine cradled in her arms. She scanned the room and followed Blade.

"Howdy," Hickok said, grinning at the couple to the left. "How's the food here?"

"Delicious," the woman answered. "Try the steak. I recommend it highly."

"Thanks. Don't mind if I do," Hickok said, stepping toward the counter.

Blade moved to within four feet of the matron. "Hello. We could use a bite to eat."

The matron beamed. "That's what I'm here for. They don't call me Ma for nothing. Tasty food and service with a smile. That's what everyone gets at my place."

Blade angled his body so he could keep an eye on the three men and the couple. "How long has your place been open?"

"Oh, about four years," Ma said. "Give or take a month."

"You get much business here?" Blade casually inquired.

"Enough," Ma replied. "We don't see much traffic heading north, but we do see a lot going toward Vegas. They're the bulk of my trade."

Hickok reached the counter and rested the Henry on top. "Howdy, Ma. Nice place you've got here."

"Why, thank you, sonny," Ma responded. "You sure are polite. What's your name?"

"The handle is Hickok," the gunman stated.

"And the big one?" Ma queried.

"That's Blade," Hickok said. "Don't mind him. His middle name is paranoia."

"And your beautiful companion?" Ma asked.

"My name is Helen," Helen said, answering for herself.

"If you don't mind my saying so, you're pretty enough to be a Vegas chorus girl," Ma mentioned appreciatively.

"What's a chorus girl?" Hickok questioned.

Ma stared at the gunman. "You mean to say you don't know what a chorus girl is? Where are you from? The moon?"

"Nope," Hickok replied.

Ma's eyes narrowed slightly. "I take it you've never been to Vegas. Anyone who's been there knows what a chorus girl is."

"Have you been to Vegas?" Blade asked.

"I was born there," Ma said.

Blade and Hickok exchanged fleeting glances.

"Do tell," the gunfighter stated. "Why don't you fix us some vittles and join us at our table? We'd like to hear all about Las Vegas."

"I'd be delighted," Ma said. "What would you like to eat?"

"How about some steaks all around," Hickok ordered. "And some milk for me, if you've got some."

"Milk?" Ma snorted. "Don't you want something stronger?"

"I never drink the hard stuff," Hickok said. "A milk will be fine."

"Milk for all of us," Blade interjected.

"It'll take about five minutes," Ma said.

"No problem," Blade told her, then walked to a table near the counter where he could command a view of Ma and the tall man behind the counter as well as the customers. He placed the Commando on the table, slid into a chair, and folded his fingers over the trigger guard.

Hickok deposited the Henry on the table, gripped the top of one of the wooden chairs and slid it to Blade's right, then reversed the chair and sat down with his arms draped over the back.

Helen took the remaining chair, sitting with her back to the front door. She leaned toward Blade. "Is it my imagination, or are these people staring at me?"

"It's not your imagination," Blade said. "They're trying not to be obvious about it, but they can't seem to take their eyes off you."

"When do you reckon they'll make their play?" Hickok asked in a hushed tone.

"What are you talking about?" Helen inquired.

Hickok lowered his voice to a whisper. "Blade was right all along. This is a trap."

Helen glanced around the room. "Are you putting me on? There's no danger here."

Blade gazed into Helen's eyes. "This is no joke. Keep your hands on your Carbine."

"How do you know this is a trap?" Helen whispered.

"Did you see the three men drinking coffee?" Blade asked.

"Of course," Helen replied.

"Did you take a look at their cups?"

"No," Helen said, and began to turn toward the men.

"Don't look at them!" Blade said hastily. "We don't want them to know we're on to them."

Helen faced the giant. "What about the coffee cups?"

"All three cups are filled to the brim, yet those men haven't taken a sip since we came in the door," Blade elaborated.

"Maybe they're not thirsty," Helen said lamely. "Maybe they've already drunk some coffee and those are their second cups. Maybe they're just waiting for their food."

"And maybe the cups are props they're usin' to try and con us," Hickok stated. "The shifty varmints!"

Helen studied the gunman for a few seconds. "I don't get you. A couple of minutes ago you were positive this diner is legit. Now you say it's a trap?"

"I knew it was a trap when I walked in the door,"

Hickok informed her.

"You didn't act like you thought it was a trap," Helen noted.

"Do you play cards?" Hickok queried.

"Cards?" Helen said, mystified. "What do cards have to do with anything?"

"A good card player never lets the other fella see his cards until it's time to put them on the table," Hickok declared.

Blade idly scanned the room. "I don't see any guns."

"They could have some stashed behind the counter," Hickok said.

Blade casually looked at the couple to the left of the door. The obese man and the woman in the red dress were simply sitting there, slight grins on their faces, their hands on top of their table, doing nothing in particular.

"You are becoming as paranoid as Blade," Helen told the gunman.

"Better paranoid than dead," Hickok retorted.

"Why don't we just walk out?" Helen proposed.

"No," Blade said. "They might let us go without any hassles, but what about the next innocent travelers who pass through Contact? What if they're not as well armed as we are?"

Helen frowned. "I don't see where this is any of our business. If you really believe it's a trap, I say we walk out and keep going. The sooner we reach Vegas, the sooner I find my daughter."

"I'm in charge," Blade reminded her. "And we're going to stay put and see what happens."

"Now what do you suppose that is all about?" Hickok asked, nodding toward the counter.

Blade turned his head, perplexed at observing Ma and the tall man embroiled in an argument. They were huddled next to a grill, speaking softly but gesturing angrily.

"Maybe they burned one of our steaks," Hickok cracked.

Blade leaned back in his chair and surveyed the room again. The "customers" were all watching the exchange between Ma and the tall man. He scrutinized their clothing, striving to detect telltale bulges that might indicate concealed firearms.

They appeared to be clean.

Ma walked to a white refrigerator and took out a pitcher of milk.

Blade abruptly realized the music had ceased minutes ago. He glanced around and found an unusual apparatus positioned against the wall six yards from the front entrance. The bottom of the machine was square, the top a golden arch. A series of bright lights rimmed the arch, reflecting off a curved glass case between the arch and the square base.

"Here we go!" Ma said happily, coming around the end of the counter with a large tray in her hands. The tray supported the pitcher and three glasses. "Here's your milk. Your steaks will be a minute or two yet."

Blade pointed at the machine with the arch. "What is that?" he inquired.

Ma set the tray on the table. "It's a jukebox. Haven't you ever seen one before?"

"No," Blade admitted.

The matron tittered. "You don't know what a chorus girl is. You don't know what a jukebox is. I've heard of pitiful, but you boys take the cake."

"You said you were born in Las Vegas," Blade remarked. "What's it like there?"

"Vegas is a tough town," Ma declared. "It's not for chumps who don't know how to take care of themselves."

"We can take care of ourselves," Hickok said, speaking up.

"You think so?" Ma rejoined.

"I know so," Hickok asserted. "Stick around. I may give you a demonstration."

"Why is Vegas a tough town?" Blade queried to get Ma back on the right track.

"Because Vegas is mob-controlled, dummy," Ma stated with a chuckle.

"You mean they have riots in the streets a lot?" Hickok asked.

Ma threw back her head and laughed. "Not that kind of a mob! I'm talking about the Families."

Blade glanced at Hickok and the gunman shrugged, signifying he didn't understand either.

The woman called Ma noticed their reaction. "Let me guess. You don't have the foggiest idea what I'm talking about, do you?"

"No," Blade answered. He was startled to learn there were other groups with the same name as the Founder's descendants.

"How do I explain it?" Ma asked herself. She stared at the giant. "Have you ever heard of Organized Crime?"

Blade reflected for a moment. The term did not ring a bell. "Never heard of it," he confessed.

Ma shook her head. "Then let me give you a refresher course. Way back when, back before the war, there were three classes of people in America. There were the ordinary slobs, rich and poor alike, who lived their lives according to the letter of the law. From cradle to grave they slaved away, basically honest jerks except for little things like cheating on their taxes and such. Oh, some of them went bad. They became drug dealers or robbed banks. But most of them were simple folks, if downright stupid." She paused and snickered. "Then there were the government types, the politicians, the most dishonest bunch of all. They stole from the people to fatten their big bellies, but they made their stealing legal. They called their system taxation. Property taxes, sales taxes, income taxes. The people were taxed to the max, and hardly complained because they trusted the politicians who were robbing them silly."

"Hold on there," Hickok interrupted. "I studied some history when I was knee-high to a grasshopper. And my teacher explained things differently. Not all politicians were crooked. There were some who cared about the people and wanted to help them. And how can you call the average folks stupid just because they obeyed the law?"

"They were stupid because they let others run their lives!" Ma replied vehemently.

Blade pursed his lips in contemplation. He had observed the woman closely as she talked. Ma wasn't the bumpkin she pretended to be, and under her seemingly friendly exterior was a heart of stone. "You mentioned there were three classes," he prompted her.

Ma smiled. "The third class was the best. They didn't pretend to be something they weren't. They knew the score. They knew there are only three things in life that matter: money, power, and loyalty. They were the organized-crime Families, and they controlled most of the action from coast to coast. The lousy politicians tried to rub the Families out, but couldn't. The Families were too strong for the government and a hell of a lot smarter. The leaders, the Dons, saw the war coming months in advance. And they decided to do something about it."

"What did they do?" Blade inquired.

"They already had a foothold in Vegas, so they decided to take the city over, lock, stock, and barrel," Ma detailed. "They flocked to Vegas right before the war began, and they were in place and ready when the crap hit the fan. When the government collapsed, it was child's play for the Families to take control. They had more soldiers in Vegas than all the law enforcement agencies combined."

"Soldiers?" Hickok said.

"Yeah. Button men. Trigger men. Hit men. They're all basically the same thing." She grinned. "So the mob has been in control of Vegas ever since. There were some rough times at first, what with the Dons unable to agree on territories and percentages. For over ten years they fought it out. The Seven Families War it's called. One Family came out on top, and their bloodline has ruled the city for seventy years. From father to son to grandson, they've passed the leadership on down the line. Their Don is the supreme Don."

"Does this Don have a name?" Blade casually asked.

Ma nodded. "The Don who runs the whole show is Don Pucci. Don Anthony Pucci."

CHAPTER FIVE

Helen's fingers gripped her Carbine until her hands started to tremble. She gritted her teeth and released the Armalite, composing her features with an effort. "Did you say Pucci?"

"Yes," Ma said. "Have you heard of him?"

Helen nodded.

Ma chuckled. "I guess everybody has heard of Don Pucci."

"What happened to the other Families?" Blade asked.

"They're still around," Ma replied. "But their Dons must take orders from Don Pucci. He makes sure they all toe the line, that they all stick to their territories and don't start any trouble."

"So the Families have divided up Vegas among them," Blade commented, pondering the implications for the mission.

Ma gazed from one Warrior to the next. "Hey! I hope nothing I've said will stop you from going to Vegas. You'll have a great time."

"We will?" Blade questioned.

"Sure," Ma stated with conviction. "Vegas is more fun

than it ever was. Thousands of people go there every year. The casinos are open around the clock. There's gambling and booze and floor shows, just like in the old days. You'll love it."

"People go there all the time?" Blade inquired.

"Thousands," Ma reiterated. "They come from Arizona, California, the Civilized Zone, everywhere. We even had some Russian officers not too long ago."

Blade straightened. "Russians in Vegas?"

"Sounds weird, doesn't it?" Ma said. "But I guess the Commies like a good time as much as the next person." She leaned over the table. "Confidentially, I heard the real reason they were in Vegas was to conduct business with Don Pucci."

"What kind of business?" Blade asked.

Ma shrugged. "Beats me. The Don doesn't fill me in on his private deals."

Blade was trying to analyze all of this new information. There were so many unanswered questions. How was it he had never heard about Vegas before? Were there really patrons coming from as far away as California and the Civilized Zone, two allies of the Family? If so, why hadn't one of their many friends told them what was happening? Surely the leaders of the Civilized Zone and California must be aware of the situation.

"You sure know a lot about Vegas," Hickok mentioned.

"I should," Ma said. "Like I told you, I was born there. I spent most of my life in Vegas, and I've been around for a long time. I'm fifty-four years old."

Blade saw the tall cook loading a tray with plates of food: steaks, potatoes, corn, and bread. He began to wonder if his suspicions were groundless. The three men at the table to the right of the door were sipping at their coffee, and the obese man and the woman in red were talking and laughing. He decided to sit tight, finish the meal, and if they weren't attacked, to leave without provoking an incident.

But one of his companions wasn't so inclined.

Helen locked her green eyes on Ma. "How long ago did the jeeps come through here?" she unexpectedly demanded.

Ma blinked her eyes rapidly several times. "Jeeps?"

"Yeah," Helen stated harshly. "You heard me. Two jeeps passed this way. I want to know how many people were in them."

Ma's lips curled downward. "I haven't seen any jeeps come by here in weeks, dearie."

Helen suddenly stood, her Carbine aimed at Ma's stomach. "Don't lie to me, bitch! I don't know what your scam is, but I know you're a liar. Those jeeps stopped here. I need to know if there was a young woman with them."

Blade picked up the Commando. All of the customers had swiveled at the sound of the dispute and were watching with intent expressions. The tall man was standing behind the counter, his hands resting on the top.

"Really, dearie," Ma said soothingly. "I don't have the faintest notion what you're talking about."

Helen's eyes flashed, her voice lowering. "I'm going to count to three. If you don't tell me what I need to know by then, I'll blow you apart."

Ma glanced at the tall man, then at Helen. "Are you nuts?"

"One," Helen said, beginning her count.

Blade was tempted to intervene, but held his tongue. Helen had started this gambit; he would do what he could to back her play.

Hickok was grinning from ear to ear, his arms draped over the back of his chair.

"Two," Helen said.

Ma looked at Blade. "Aren't you going to do anything? Are you just going to sit there and let her shoot me?"

"If I were you," Blade advised, "I'd tell her what she wants to know."

Ma clenched her fists and glared at Helen. "There's only one thing I've got to say to you!" she snapped. "Go to hell!"

"Three," Helen stated somberly.

Ma abruptly performed a remarkable maneuver. She executed a dive for the floor while bawling at the top of her lungs, "Get them!"

Blade saw the tall man behind the counter bringing a shotgun up, and he threw himself backward so Hickok wouldn't be in his line of fire. He squeezed the trigger as he fell, and the Commando thundered and bucked in his brawny hands.

The tall man was caught in the chest and flung from sight.

Blade landed on his back and swiveled to find the customers producing handguns with astonishing swiftness, as if from thin air. But fast as they were, the Family's preeminent gunfighter was faster.

Hickok came up off his chair with his arms a blurred streak, drawing his Pythons with ambidextrous precision. The Colts boomed three times in succession, the shots spaced so close together they sounded as one, and the three men to the right of the front door went down, each one struck in the head, each dying soundlessly, one of them sprawling over the table while the other two toppled to the floor.

The obese man and the woman in red were taking a bead on the Warriors when Helen cut loose. Her carbine chattered, the slugs ripping into the heavyset man and doubling him over. The woman in red got off a solitary harmless round, and then she was propelled backwards by a burst to her face. She crashed onto a chair and slumped down. The obese man, gurgling and wheezing, staggered a few steps, then pitched forward.

Silence momentarily descended.

Blade leaped to his feet, scrutinizing the bodies to insure none of their foes were moving.

"A piece of cake!" Hickok declared, grinning.

"Check them," Blade ordered.

The gunman walked toward the nearest corpse to verify the man was dead.

Ma was on her hands and knees, gawking at her dead comrades in amazement.

Helen walked around the table and grabbed Ma by the right shoulder. "On your feet!" she commanded, hauling the matron erect.

Ma glanced toward the counter. "Poor Harry! He was right! I should have listened to him."

"Right about what?" Blade demanded.

Ma looked at the giant. "He said we shouldn't mess with you. He said you were trouble. He was right."

Helen jabbed her carbine barrel to within an inch of Ma's nose. "I want some answers, woman, and I want them now!"

Ma gulped. "Whatever you want, dearie."

"I want to know about the two jeeps," Helen stated.

Ma began fidgeting with her apron. "The two jeeps?"

Helen's eyes narrowed menacingly. "Don't play games with me! Two jeeps came by here recently. When?"

"Yesterday morning," Ma answered.

"Was there a young woman in one of them?" Helen queried anxiously.

"Let me see," Ma said reflectively, pursing her lips. "I seem to recall about six or seven men. They pulled in and ordered some food to go."

Helen placed the tip of the carbine barrel against Ma's forehead. "You'd better remember more than that."

Ma was wringing her hands in the apron. "Yes! I do! Now that I think about it, there was a woman with them. She used the facilities."

"Describe her!" Helen directed.

"Well, I didn't pay all that much attention," Ma said. "But I think she had red hair and was wearing a green blouse. I don't remember the color of her pants."

"Did you talk to her?" Helen inquired, lowering the carbine.

Ma shook her head. "Like I said, they pulled in and ordered some food to go. I saw them through the window, standing next to the jeeps and stretching their legs. Two of them came in and ordered the food. And two of them went with the young lady and waited outside the door while she did her business."

Hickok strolled over, his Pythons in his hands. "They're all fit for the vultures," he said.

Ma glanced at the gunman. "I've got to hand it to you, sonny. I've lived a long time, and I've seen my share of men who fancied themselves quick with a gun, but I'ver never seen anyone the likes of you."

Hickok chuckled. "Just natural aptitude, I reckon."

Blade crossed to the counter and peered over the rim. The tall man was crumpled on the floor, blood oozing from a half-dozen holes. He turned and studied the matron. "What was the setup here?"

"Setup?" Ma repeated innocently.

"Whatever it was," Hickok mentioned, "it was mighty slick. Those cow chips had their handguns taped underneath their tables."

Blade walked up to Ma. "What was the setup? Did your gang rob the customers who came through?"

Ma snorted. "I wouldn't stay in business long if I did that, now would I? Besides, I wouldn't stoop to petty robbery."

"Then what was it?" Blade snapped.

"I'm in the skin trade," Ma said.

"The what?" Blade responded.

"Oh. I keep forgetting. You don't know a thing about Vegas," Ma said. "So let me fill you in. There are dozens of casinos in Vegas. And for every casino there are five houses—"

"Houses?" Blade interrupted.

"Yeah. You know. Brothels. Whorehouses," Ma stated. "Houses of prostitution."

"Prostitu—" Blade began in astonishment.

"Yeah. Don't tell me you don't know what a prostitute is?" Ma asked.

"I've read about them," Blade admitted.

"*Read* about them?" Ma said, then laughed. "You've never visited a whorehouse?"

"No," Blade replied.

"Now I know you're from the moon!" Ma quipped.

"What do these whorehouses and the casinos have to do

with your setup?" Blade questioned.

"I'm in the skin trade," Ma explained. "There aren't as many women around as there used to be. The houses and the casinos need women. Pretty women. Lots and lots of them. I'm in the supply business. If a real looker comes along, like your friend here, I arrange to send her to Vegas."

"How do you arrange it?" Blade probed.

Ma nodded at the tray of milk on the table. "Usually we drug their drinks. When they pass out, we grab them. Easy as pie."

"But what if there are others with them? What if they're with their family?" Blade inquired.

"They're taken care of," Ma said.

"You mean they're killed," Blade deduced.

Ma didn't respond.

Helen's lips curled downward distastefully. "You drug women and force them into a life of prostitution? How could you?"

"Don't look down your nose at me, dearie!" Ma rejoined. "Being a pro isn't as bad as all that. I should know. I worked the line once, I worked my way up to become the madam at one of the top casinos in Vegas. But there comes a time when you get put out to pasture, when you get too old for the trade. So when Don Giorgio offered me this franchise, I could hardly refuse. I make a good living here."

"Who is Don Giorgio?" Blade asked.

"He's the head of the second most powerful Family in Vegas," Ma answered.

"How long have you been doing this?" Blade queried.

"Four years," Ma said.

"So you planned to drug us and sell me into prostitution?" Helen wanted to know.

"I was going to do it," Ma admitted, "but Harry talked me out of the idea. He said you were packing too much hardware, that you looked like you could handle yourselves. He said you were professionals, that we should let you leave in peace. So I agreed. Harry was always a shrewd judge of character." She paused and snickered. "Isn't this funny? We decide not to try and snatch Helen, we don't even bother to drug your drinks, and you end up blowing most of us away!"

"It's hilarious," Blade said dryly.

"We should head on out," Helen urged. "Mindy must be in Vegas by now."

"Tell me something," Ma said to Helen. "What's this girl to you?"

Helen's features hardened. "She's my daughter."

Ma did a double take. "I didn't know."

Hickok pointed at Ma. "What are we going to do about her? If we let her live, she might find a way of lettin' the bigwigs in Vegas know we're comin'."

Ma, her hands buried in her apron, looked at Blade. "I won't rat! Honest!"

Blade stared at the matron. What *were* they going to do? If they tied her up and left her at the diner, someone was bound to come along, find her, and let her loose. Taking her with them wasn't feasible either. One of them would need to watch her at all times, and he couldn't spare anyone for the job.

The matter was suddenly taken out of his hands.

Helen absently lowered her carbine to her side, gazing at the matron with a slight grin on her face. "Now I want you to tell me something," she said.

"What's that, dearie?" Ma responded.

Helen smiled sweetly. "I'd like to know what's in that apron of yours?"

Ma stiffened. "There's nothing in my apron."

"Prove it," Helen stated.

Blade saw Ma sweep her right hand from under her apron, and he detected the metallic glint of a gun even as he brought the Commando up. But before he could squeeze the trigger, Helen fired. Her slugs slammed into the matron's neck and face, and Ma was hurled backwards to tumble over a chair.

Ma wound up on her right side, crimson spurting from

her throat and mouth, a derringer clutched in her lifeless right hand.

Helen walked over to the matron and nudged the body with her right boot. "She got what she deserved!" she snapped.

"Nice shootin'," Hickok said. "I was going to plug her myself, but I figured you should have the honor."

Helen looked at Blade. "Can we take off now?"

"In a minute," Blade told her. "We must settle some things first." He paused. "Who's in charge here?"

"You are," Helen replied promptly.

"Who decides when we will fight and when we won't?" Blade asked.

"You do," Helen said.

"Then why did you start this?" Blade demanded. "You didn't even believe this was a trap when we suggested it."

Helen gazed at Ma's corpse. "I got to thinking about the things Hickok and you said. I realized you were right. And the more I watched Ma, the more convinced I became that she knew something about Mindy. When she mentioned Don Pucci, that clinched it. I'm sorry. I was way out of line. I should have waited for your signal. It won't happen again."

"It better not," Blade cautioned. He surveyed the diner. "Let's head for Vegas before someone else shows up. They'll never know who did this if they're aren't any witnesses."

Helen hefted her Carbine. "I should be honest with you."

"How so?" Blade responded.

"I'll try to follow your orders at all times," Helen said. "But when we get to Vegas, if we find Mindy has been hurt or been forced to become a . . . a prostitute, then I intend to kill everyone responsible. With or without your permission." She stalked toward the front door.

Blade sighed in annoyance. He should have expected this attitude. Helen was too emotionally involved with the mission to function effectively. He should never have agreed to bring her along.

Hickok was reloading the spent rounds in his Pythons, smiling impishly.

"What's so funny?" Blade asked.

"Helen," Hickok replied.

"What about her?"

Hickok watched her walk out the door. "I never realized it before, but the lady is a lot like me."

"As if I didn't have enough to worry about," Blade muttered.

CHAPTER SIX

"Here he comes," Hickok announced.

Blade saw him too. Geronimo was 500 yards off, jogging up the hill toward the stand of trees and brush in which the SEAL was concealed.

"I don't know how wise it is to leave the SEAL here when we go into Vegas," Helen commented from the giant's left.

Blade glanced at her. "There you go again."

"But we'd be safer in the SEAL," Helen said. "It's bulletproof."

"It would also stand out like a sore thumb," Blade told her. "We've seen over a hundred cars and trucks enter Vegas since we pulled into these trees. But the SEAL is unique. There's nothing else like it. We'd attract too much attention if we take it into Vegas. So we'll go in on foot." He stared at the buildings to the southwest. Only an hour ago they had driven over a rise and spied the city approximately a mile distant. He had continued on until he'd spotted a suitable site to camouflage the transport, then wheeled off the road after checking to guarantee no one was coming from either direction. Now, as he waited for Geronimo to reach them, he double-checked the makeshift latticework of branches and brush they had used to hide the SEAL.

"Las Vegas is huge," Helen remarked with a touch of trepidation. "How will we ever find Mindy in there?"

Blade adjusted a large limb over the SEAL's grill. "We'll find her," he vowed.

"Do you have a plan?" Helen asked hopefully.

"We'll play it by ear," Blade said.

"That's a plan?" Helen retorted.

Blade gazed at her. "Do you have a better idea?"

"I sure do," Helen stated. "You said Mindy will be at the Golden Crown Casino, right?"

"That's what Ted was told," Blade confirmed.

"Then I say we march right into the Golden Crown Casino and get her back!" Helen declared.

"No," Blade said.

"Why not?" Helen demanded.

"Will you think with your head instead of your heart?" Blade responded. "They will be expecting us to do exactly like you propose. They'll be waiting for us. And what good can we do Mindy if we walk into a trap?"

"We can't leave her in their hands!" Helen objected.

"I don't intend to leave Mindy in their hands a second more than is absolutely necessary," Blade said. "But we'll take it slow at first. We'll mingle, walk around, act like everybody else, blend right in. Hopefully, we can discover the extent of our opposition."

"Whatever you say," Helen commented halfheartedly.

Blade moved around the transport, carefully inspecting the camouflage.

Helen's shoulders slumped as she faced Las Vegas. She noticed Hickok was to her right, leaning against a tree, staring at her. "What are you looking at?" she snapped.

"I'm admirin' your fortitude," the gunfighter said.

Helen studied him for a moment, trying to determine if the gunman was serious. He was.

"I also wanted to apologize for the crack I made about

your husband," Hickok said sincerely. "It was a boneheaded thing to say, but you did get me all riled up."

"I guess I had it coming," Helen said.

"I had no right to comment on your personal life," Hickok mentioned. "I was just fed up with your gripin'."

Helen looked up at the blue morning sky. "I can't believe how I'm acting on this trip!" she remarked pensively. "I pride myself on my self-control, but I certainly haven't exhibited any."

"Who can blame you?" Hickok said. "If my son was down there, I'd go crazy."

Helen sighed. "Mindy is all I have left in this world. My parents died about six years ago. Then Andy left me for another woman. Talk about creating a scandal! We were the talk of the Home for months! Divorces are extremely rare in the Family. You know that. I'm sure you heard all the gossip."

"I heard it," Hickok said softly.

"I was heartbroken," Helen divulged. "I loved Andy. Truly loved him. I was stunned when he told me he wanted a divorce. He claimed I was stifling his manhood. Can you imagine that?" She laughed bitterly. "We appeared before the Elders, and he stood there and read a list of reasons for our marital failure, as he called it. I was too bossy. I was a dictator. I couldn't relate to him as a woman. I was immature. I was spiritually stagnant." She stopped and closed her eyes. "According to him, I was the worst woman imaginable. I suppose I shouldn't have been surprised when the Elders granted his divorce petition, but I was."

"The Elders were right to grant the petition," Hickok stated.

Helen's eyes opened and she glanced at the gunman. "Oh? So you believe Andy was telling the truth?"

"I believe Andy is a wimp," Hickok declared. "Always has been. And when you pair a wimp with a strong person in a marriage, either the wimp grows up and they learn to share as equals, or the strong person always dominates the marriage, or the wimp cracks under the pressure. The

Elders knew Andy couldn't handle the responsibility of being your hubby. If Andy had stayed with you, he would have made your life miserable. He was already foolin' around with Gladys before he even asked you for a divorce. And let's face it. Gladys is a ding-a-ling. Andy and her are perfect for each other. He wasn't mature enough for a real woman like you."

Helen grinned. "You missed your calling. You should have been a Counselor."

Blade came around the transport. "The SEAL is locked tight as a drum." He walked forward several yards, his eyes on Geronimo, who was now less than 20 feet away.

"About time you got here," Hickok declared loudly. "Married life has made you flabby."

Geronimo reached them and halted, breathing easily. "The only flab around here is between your ears," he said to Hickok, then faced Blade.

"What did you find out?" Blade asked.

"Anyone can come and go as they like," Geronimo reported. "The road leads straight into the heart of Las Vegas. There are thousands of people everywhere."

"Any checkpoints or security forces?" Blade inquired.

Geronimo shook his head. "Not a one. The city is wide open. And get this. Carrying firearms must be legal because many of the people I saw were armed. Men and women alike. I went about a quarter of a mile into the city, and I wasn't stopped or challenged once."

"Then we go in," Blade stated. "And we stay close together."

"Are you going to carry me piggyback?" Hickok joked.

Blade led them down the hill, angling toward the road, scanning the area for other travelers. The hill was 600 yards from the highway, and he felt supremely confident the transport would not be discovered. Nevertheless, he didn't want anyone to observe the Warriors emerging from the brush. Whenever a car or truck appeared on the road he flattened and the others followed his lead. They reached the highway without being seen, coming out near the point where the SEAL had left the road.

"Blade," Geronimo said. "Look!" He pointed at a spot ten feet off.

Blade turned and saw them: the tracks the SEAL's massive wheels had made in the field bordering the highway. The huge tires had crushed the grass and weeds.

"Should we try to cover them up?" Geronimo inquired.

Blade heard a low rumble and spied a car approaching from the southwest, leaving Las Vegas. "No. I doubt anyone will pay much attention to the tracks. They may assume someone pulled off for a rest stop. If we try to cover them, everyone driving by will see us. We'd arouse more curiosity than the tracks themselves. Let's go." He marched to the southwest. The car sped past them.

Geronimo fell in behind his giant friend.

Hickok and Helen brought up the rear.

"You must be on pins and needles," the gunman commented.

Helen managed a feeble smile. "You don't know the half of it."

"Just remember you're not in this alone," Hickok said. "We'll help you get Mindy out."

Helen stared at the buckskin-clad gunfighter. "You're not what I expected," she remarked.

"I'm not?" Hickok responded.

"Definitely not," Helen declared. "We haven't had occasion to talk together very frequently. My estimation of you was based on all the stories circulating around the Family, and the stories don't do justice to your personality."

"In what way?" Hickok inquired.

"In every way," Helen said. "According to the tales I heard, you're just about the deadliest Warrior. Your courage is indisputable, but you're also a bit of a blockhead. You have no regard for your personal safety. You'll walk into a hot spot without batting an eye, and you'll rely on your speed to bail you out if you get in over your head. Your motto is, 'Shoot first and ask questions later,' and you always go for the head. Some of the Family think you're too reckless, others believe you're the Warrior who always gets the job done, no matter what the odds might be. Personally, I don't think you're as big a blockhead as some people claim."

"Thanks," Hickok stated. "I think."

"You're more intelligent and understanding than most give you credit for being," Helen observed. "I'm beginning to see why Sherry married you."

Hickok smirked. "She's in love with my dimples."

Geronimo glanced over his left shoulder at Helen. "Don't let him kid you. The only reason Sherry married him was because he brainwashed her. Somehow he convinced her he's an ordinary kind of guy. If I didn't know better, I'd swear he hypnotized her."

"Can I help it if the Spirit blessed me with charm, wit, and good looks?" Hickok queried lightheartedly.

"Don't forget modesty," Geronimo added.

Another car passed them, heading to the northeast.

Blade trained his eyes on the buildings ahead. Even though it was daytime, with bright sunshine, there seemed to be a lot of lights on in Vegas. Most were neon lights advertising businesses: casinos, hotels, motels, and the like. As they drew nearer he could see the throngs of people packing the sidewalks. Vehicle traffic was also surprisingly heavy.

Geronimo took two hasty strides and caught up with Blade. "See? No checkpoints, police, nothing."

"Maybe they don't need a police force," Blade speculated. "Maybe they don't want one. Ma said Organized Crime controls the entire city, and I doubt the mob would allow a police force to exist."

"But how do they keep the crowds under control?" Geronimo asked. "With all the gambling, and the drinking, and the womanizing that goes on here, there must be problems with drunks and other rowdy types. How does the mob keep them in line?"

"I imagine we'll find out," Blade said.

They reached the first buildings, sleazy motels on both sides of the highway. A wide sidewalk bordered the front of the motel nearest them.

Blade gazed across the highway and noted another sidewalk on the opposite side. The motels were doing a thriving business; vehicles were pulling in and out of the motel parking lots every few seconds. He was puzzled by the heavy traffic until he saw one of the cars pull up to a door labeled FRONT OFFICE. A lean man in a green suit stood outside the Front Office door. Whenever a vehicle pulled up alongside him, the driver would hand the man money and the man would give the driver a small white packet.

"What is that all about?" Geronimo inquired, watching yet another transaction.

"I don't know," Blade said.

"Want me to find out, pard?" Hickok offered.

"No," Blade replied. "I don't want any of us making waves. We don't want to do anything to get ourselves noticed. We have a better chance of finding Mindy if we don't draw attention to us."

They entered Las Vegas.

And three minutes later attracted exactly the attention Blade didn't want.

CHAPTER SEVEN

Blade was extremely pleased.

None of the predestrians paid any attention to the four Warriors. The hustling crowds flowed to and fro, from casino to motel or liquor store, a frenetic swirl of humanity composed of frontier types in buckskins, Las Vegas residents and tourists in shirts and slacks or shorts, and dapper sorts in three-piece suits. Machine guns, rifles, and handguns were in abundance.

The Warriors fit right in.

Blade did notice the stares Helen was receiving from many of the men. But dozens of beautiful women were strolling along the sidewalk, each one the focus of masculine interest. The women wore skimpy tops and short, short skirts, and they flaunted their sexuality with a pronounced swaying of their hips and the suggestive contours of their breasts.

"Hey! Look!" Hickok said. "That sign."

Blade halted in midstride in front of a liquor store. To the right of the entrance was a large white sign with black lettering. "Let's read it," he stated.

They crossed the parking lot and walked up to the sign.

WELCOME TO LAS VEGAS

The recreation capital of the Western Hemisphere! If we don't have it, you don't need it! All establishments are open twenty-four hours a day for your enjoyment and convenience. Precious metals and jewelry are accepted at any Exchange Center in every casino. Prewar currency is also acceptable at the current rate of exchange. Firearms are permitted, but the killing of unarmed tourists is strictly forbidden. Las Vegas thrives on its tourist trade. Any violations will be dealt with by the Enforcers. All questions will be courteously answered at any of the Information Booths. Thank you for vacationing in Las Vegas! We hope to see you again next year!

The Las Vegas Chamber

"Friendly folks hereabouts," Hickok remarked.

"Who are the Enforcers?" Geronimo queried.

"Your guess is as good as mine," Blade responded. "Let's keep moving."

The four Warriors turned.

Just as the front door to the liquor store opened and five men walked out. All five wore suits and three wore hats. Two of them carried Uzi submachine guns. The apparent leader was a stocky man with a pockmarked face who was wearing a blue pin-striped suit and a white hat. In his right hand was a bottle of whiskey. He started to take a swig as he headed toward a parked red sedan. His brown eyes alighted on the Warriors and he stopped. "Whoa! What have we here?"

"Uh-oh," Geronimo mumbled. "We've got trouble."

The man in the white hat cocked his head to one side, lustfully gazing at Helen. "Do you see what I see, Reggie?"

One of the men with an Uzi, a tall man in a tan suit, nodded. "I see her, Franky."

Franky took a sip of whiskey and walked toward the Warriors, flanked by his four henchmen.

Blade was standing slightly ahead of his companions. He took a stride forward, the Commando held at waist height. "Do you want something?"

Franky halted, lowering the bottle and warily studying the giant. "This doesn't concern you, buddy!"

"I think it does," Blade stated.

Franky nodded toward Helen. "I want a few words with the fox."

"About what?" Blade asked.

"That's between the broad and me!" Franky declared testily.

"What do you want?" Helen spoke up.

Franky smirked. "I want to show you a good time, gorgeous. Why don't you dump these assholes and come with me? You'll see the sights in style."

"No, thanks," Helen said politely.

Franky's eyes narrowed. "Don't you know who I am?"

"Nope," Helen replied. "And I don't care."

Franky seemed insulted. He glanced at the one named Reggie. "Tell this bimbo who I am!"

"You don't want to mess with Franky, lady," Reggie warned. "He's connected."

"Connected to what? That bottle?" Helen retorted.

Franky hissed and angrily tossed the bottle to the pavement. The bottle shattered, spraying whiskey in all directions. "I'm a made man, bitch! Does the name Giorgio mean anything to you?"

"Should it?" Helen rejoined.

Blade suddenly recalled the matron at the diner mentioning Don Giorgio. What had she said? Something about Don Giorgio being the head of the second most powerful Family in Vegas.

"Do you know who my old man is?" Franky asked belligerently.

"I do," Blade said. "And we don't want any trouble with you."

Franky grinned cockily. "Oh, really? Well, Jerkface,

you'll have more trouble than you can handle if Sweet-Cheeks doesn't come for a ride with me."

Hickok abruptly stepped to the right, slinging the Henry over his left shoulder.

The four men with Franky shifted their attention to the gunman.

Hickok's hands dropped to his sides and he grinned.

"What's so funny, Ugly?" Franky snapped.

Blade tried one more time to prevent bloodshed. "We don't want any trouble with you. Just let us walk away in peace."

Franky snorted contemptuously. "The only way you'll leave is in pieces."

Blade realized pedestrians had gathered on the sidewalk and were watching in fascination. He saw the two henchmen with Uzis fingering their weapons. The other three had swept their jackets aside to reveal pistols stuck under their belts. With a sinking feeling he knew there would be gunplay.

"So what's it going to be?" Franky demanded. "Do you hand over the vixen or do we whack you?"

"How do you do it?" Hickok unexpectedly queried.

Franky stared at the man in buckskins. "Do what, hick?"

"I've never seen anyone with your talent," Hickok mentioned.

Franky moved the right side of his jacket aside, his hand moving to within an inch of an automatic. "What the hell are you talking about?"

"I've never met anyone who could fart out of their mouth before," Hickok said. "How do you do it?"

Several seconds elapsed before Franky's alcohol-benumbed mind perceived he had been insulted. With a snarl he grabbed for this gun.

Hickok was the first to fire. The Colts flashed from their holsters and boomed, the twin shots as one.

Franky took both shots in the head, one in each eye, his cranium bursting outwards, his brains and blood gushing over the asphalt as he was flung backwards.

Hickok swiveled before Franky started to fall, planting two more shots into one of the henchmen.

Reggie swung his Uzi toward the gunfighter, but he died before he could squeeze the trigger. A burst from the giant's machine gun ripped into his abdomen and nearly tore him in half. He crumpled to the ground, the Uzi slipping from his fingers, his consciousness slowly fading, agony wracking his body. Doubled over, on his knees, shock overwhelming his senses, he saw the fight end as swiftly as it began. The giant spun and took out Lou with another skillful burst to Lou's chest, even as the Indian and the fox shot Berk and Clemens. Reggie sagged, blood spouting from his gaping mouth, his eyes glazing. A pair of moccasins appeared in his line of vision and he craned his neck upward.

"Howdy," the man in the buckskin said. "Your pards are done for. Any last words before I put you out of your misery?"

Reggie used the last of his strength to spit out, "Get screwed!"

Hickok shrugged, extending both Pythons. "I figured you might want to make your peace with your Maker." He cocked the Colts. "I reckon I was wrong." He fired, the Pythons blasting, Reggie's forehead caving inward as the two heavy slugs plowed through his brain.

Reggie toppled onto the asphalt.

Hickok glanced at his friends. "Anyone hit?"

"I'm fine," Geronimo answered.

"Ditto," Helen said.

Blade walked up to Franky's corpse. "I hope we don't run into more idiots like this one."

There was a commotion in the crowd on the sidewalk.

Blade faced the pedestrians, ready to cut loose if they displayed any hostility. To his amazement, none of the people crowding the sidewalk showed any hint of anger or resentment. The commotion was being caused by several men striving to reach the liquor store parking lot.

Were these newcomers associates of Franky's?"

The three men finally pressed through the throng and

stopped. All three wore dark-colored suits; each one was armed with a machine gun. One of them, a burly man with a black mustache and a hooked nose, walked toward the Warriors, his dark eyes surveying the five corpses gravely. "Damn!" he exclaimed when he spied Franky's body.

Hickok, Geronimo, and Helen were keeping the three men covered.

The man with the mustache looked up at Blade. "Do you know what you've done?"

"They started it," Blade said.

The man twisted toward the sidewalk. "How about it? Who saw this? Who started it?"

"Franky did," a man called out.

"Yeah," declared a woman in a red skirt. "We saw the whole thing. They told Franky they didn't want no trouble. Franky wouldn't listen."

"He finally bit off more than he could chew!" someone quipped.

"Then it was a fair and square?" the man with the mustache questioned them.

A half dozen or so nodded. A few yelled out, "Yes!"

"My name is DePetrillo," the man with the mustache stated. "I head one of the Enforcer squads. It's my job to report every killing. If it's a fair and square, there's no problem. But if it's done dirty, if unarmed civilians are shot, then a dozen Enforcers go after the guilty party." He paused and gazed at Franky, then sighed. "This is trouble, mister. What's your name?"

"George Smith," Blade lied.

"Why are you in Vegas?" DePetrillo inquired.

"We came to see the sights," Blade replied.

DePetrillo frowned. "Is this your first time in Vegas?"

"Yes," Blade admitted.

"Then let me set you straight," DePetrillo said. "Ordinarily, there's no beef over a fair and square. But one of the men you killed was Franky Giorgio. I never liked Franky much myself. He was all mouth. But he was also the son of Johnny Giorgio, and Johnny is one of the most powerful men in Vegas. I'll report this as a fair and square to Don Pucci, but even Don Pucci might not be able to keep Giorgio in line over the killing of his son. Giorgio may ask for a sanction to whack you. Do you understand me?"

"I think so," Blade said. "You're warning me that Giorgio may come after us."

DePetrillo nodded. "If I were you, I'd haul ass out of Vegas right now."

"We can't," Blade said.

"Suit yourself," DePetrillo stated. "But don't say I didn't warn you. Now get out of here before some of Giorgio's boys show up."

Blade motioned for his three fellow Warriors to follow. "Thanks," he said as he passed DePetrillo.

The Enforcer scrutinized the giant. "Don't thank me, mister. I'm just doing my job."

The crowd parted to permit the Warriors access to the sidewalk.

Blade resumed their trek into the heart of the city. He replaced the clip in his Commando.

Hickok, busily reloading his Colts, reached Blade's right side. "George Smith, huh? Now there's an original name!"

"I couldn't very well give my real name," Blade said. "Pucci is expecting the Warriors to try and rescue Mindy. But he doesn't know when. He gave us a month, remember? If I gave my real name to that Enforcer, Don Pucci would know we're in Vegas now. I want to surprise him."

"I'm partial to the direct approach," Hickok mentioned.

"I know," Blade agreed.

"So why don't we find Don Pucci, shove a gun down his throat, and give him five seconds to turn Mindy over or else?" Hickok suggested.

"Be serious," Blade said. "Don Pucci will be guarded by his button men, as Ma called them. I doubt anyone can get close to Pucci without an appointment. And I can't see him giving me an appointment."

"I still don't understand why Pucci took Mindy," Hickok remarked. "Why lure us all the way to Vegas? And why did Pucci ask for you by name?"

"I wish I knew," Blade responded.

CHAPTER EIGHT

"We're being followed," Geronimo announced.

Blade knew better than to turn around and search for their tail. "Where?" he casually inquired over his right shoulder.

"About forty yards behind us," Geronimo said. "There are two of them. They've been shadowing us for two or three minutes."

"Are they armed?" Blade queried.

"I don't see any rifles or machine guns," Geronimo responded. "But they could have handguns concealed under their jackets. They're both wearing dark suits."

"What's the plan, Big Guy?" Hickok asked.

Blade pondered their next move. He estimated they were over a mile from the liquor store. Ahead was a stretch of highway with casino after casino on both sides. Secondary streets periodically intersected the main thoroughfare. More people than ever before jammed the sidewalks, and the vehicle traffic was bumper to bumper.

"Want me to take care of them?" Hickok proposed.

"We'll do it my way," Blade said. "Come on." He

walked to the nearest intersection and waited at the curb with a crowd of pedestrians until the traffic light displayed a WALK sign.

The Warriors quickly crossed.

Blade was hoping his strategy would work. They had traversed six intersections since leaving the liquor store, and he had noticed the traffic lights never flashed the WALK sign for more than 30 seconds. Anyone wanting to cross was compelled to walk rapidly. The two men following the Warriors would be unable to catch up until the next light change. He hoped.

"They didn't make it," Geronimo confirmed, idly gazing to their rear.

Blade increased his pace, searching for the ideal spot.

Geronimo, faking an interest in the casinos, scanned the structures to the rear. "The light still hasn't changed," he mentioned.

An alley appeared to the right.

Blade slowed, noting the crates stacked at the mouth of the alley, partially obscuring the entrance. "Where are they?"

"Still waiting for the light," Geronimo said.

"Into this alley then," Blade instructed them, and took a right when he reached it. The alley was littered with refuse and lined with metal trash cans.

"Yuck!" Hickok declared. "What a smell!"

"Reminds me of you before your annual bath," Geronimo quipped.

Blade saw an open door 15 feet away. He cautiously advanced and peered inside, discovering a gloomy corridor with a closed door at the far end. "In here," he ordered, then stood aside so they could file into the hallway.

"I don't like being cooped up like this," Hickok commented.

Blade stepped inside and drew the door shut until only a crack remained, enough visibility to afford him a view of the alley mouth and the stretch up to the door.

"Are you aimin' to jump these clowns?" Hickok asked.

"I am," Blade verified, peeking through the crack.

Hickok chuckled. "This is another thing I like about Las Vegas. There's never a dull moment."

Blade watched the mouth of the alley for their shadows. Seconds later two men in dark suits, with felt hats, reached the entrance and paused uncertainly. Blade knew they were perplexed. He doubted the pair had seen the Warriors enter the alley, so they must be wondering how the Warriors could have vanished into thin air.

The two men became embroiled in a heated exchange.

Blade grinned. One of the men, the skinniest, was gesturing along the main drag, indicating he wanted to stick to the highway. But the other one was jabbing his right thumb toward the alley, apparently arguing the alley should be checked before they proceeded.

The skinny one lost.

Both men walked into the alley.

Blade slung his Commando over his broad back and drew his right Bowie. "Geronimo," he whispered. "Take the skinny one."

Geronimo nodded, then handed the Browning to Helen. He slid his tomahawk from under his belt.

Blade tensed as the second man, a pale, mousy man not over five feet tall, approached the door. He waited until the last possible instant, until the mousy mobster was reaching for the doorknob, before he lunged, ramming his powerful right shoulder into the door and sending it flying wide.

Startled, the mousy mobster was caught off guard. The door struck him in the chest and knocked him onto the ground.

Blade was on the mobster like a pouncing panther. He leaped and landed with his right knee folded, his leg hard, ramming the knee into the mobster's abdomen. The man grunted and turned red, gasping for air.

The skinny one reacted incredibly swiftly, his left hand going for a Smith and Wesson tucked in his waistband. He never pulled it.

Geronimo reached the skinny mobster in three bounds, the tomahawk glinting in the sunlight. He delivered a resounding blow to the left side of the mobster's head with the flat of his weapon, splitting the skin and staggering the mobster but leaving the skinny man alive.

Blade placed the point of his right Bowie next to the mousy mobster's left eye. "Why were you following us?" he demanded.

"Wasn't . . ." the man replied, wheezing.

Hickok and Helen moved past Blade and Geronimo to cover the alley entrance.

"I won't ask again," Blade stated harshly. "Who are you? Why were you following us?"

"I wasn't!" Mousy replied angrily.

Blade cut him. He slashed the Bowie across the man's left cheek, leaving an inch-deep slit.

Mousy started to shriek.

Blade pressed his left hand over Mousy's mouth. "Don't make a sound or you're dead!"

Mousy's brown eyes widened fearfully.

Blade looked up. Hickok and Helen were near the alley mouth, blocking the view of the passersby. Skinny was clutching the wound to his head, blood seeping over his fingers. The mobster's hat had fallen to the ground. Geronimo held the tomahawk aloft, prepared to strike again if necessary.

Perfect.

He could concentrate on his interrogation.

Blade grinned down at the small mobster. "Now you were saying? Why were you following us?" He lifted his left hand.

Mousy took a gulp of putrid alley air. "Told to!" he blurted. "Orders!"

"Orders from whom?" Blade demanded.

"Orders from Kenney," Mousy disclosed.

"And who is Kenney?" Blade queried.

"Kenney is Don Giorgio's right-hand man," Mousy explained. "We were at the casino a while ago when a call came in. Somebody whacked Giorgio's son, Franky—"

"I know," Blade interrupted. "We did."

"You admit it?" Mousy asked in astonishment. "You

must be wacko!"

"Keep talking," Blade stated.

"Kenney got a description of you guys," Mousy detailed. "He told us to tail you. We cruised the strip until I spotted you, then we parked and tailed you on foot."

"What were you supposed to do? Kill us?" Blade inquired.

"Just follow you," Mousy said.

Blade smirked. "Why don't I believe you?"

"Honest!" Mousy asserted. "We were ordered to follow you, make a note of places you stopped at and the people you talked to, and call in a report every hour."

"Does Giorgio want revenge for the death of his son?" Blade asked.

"I haven't talked to Don Giorgio," Mousy replied. "I talked to Kenney. But if you're asking my opinion, yeah. Giorgio won't stand still for the racking of Franky. He'll probably ask Don Pucci for a sanction to snuff you guys."

"We don't want to fight Don Giorgio," Blade commented.

"I'll bet you don't!" Mousy said scornfully.

"Can you tell him that?" Blade queried.

"Sure," Mousy responded. "But it won't do no good. You killed his son. Blood talks, you know."

"And there's nothing I could say or do to convince Don Giorgio to leave us alone?" Blade questioned.

"Leave you alone? Not on your life!" Mousy declared.

Blade frowned, irritated by the turn of events. As if rescuing Mindy wasn't enough of a problem, now he had to contend with a vengeful Don!

"You've got two choices," Mousy said. "You can play it smart and get the hell out of Vegas, or you can stay and die. It's that simple."

"There's one more option," Blade noted.

"What's that?" Mousy asked.

"I can kill Don Giorgio if he doesn't leave us alone," Blade stated.

Despite his wounded left cheek, Mousy laughed. "Kill Don Giorgio? You're out of your mind!"

Blade slowly stood. "Where is Giorgio's headquarters?"

"Where else? The Don hangs out at his place," Mousy divulged. "He has his own casino, just like all the other Dons."

"What's the name of Giorgio's casino?" Blade demanded.

"Johnny's Palace," Mousy answered.

Blade's eyes narrowed. "One more question. Where does Don Pucci hang out?"

"At the Golden Crown Casino, mostly," Mousy said. "Why?"

"None of your business," Blade replied. "On your feet."

Mousy complied.

Blade wagged his right Bowie in front of the mobster's eyes. "I want you to relay a message to Don Giorgio. Tell him I'm coming after him."

"You're what?" Mousy blurted in disbelief.

"Tell Giorgio I'm coming after him since he can't leave well enough alone," Blade directed. "Tell him I'll be at his Palace soon."

Mousy's mouth dropped. "You won't last three seconds."

"Just tell him," Blade snapped. "And tell him this. If he's a man and not a coward, he'll meet me one on one."

Mousy made a clucking sound. "What a jerk! I'll relay your message, and I hope I'm there when the Don creams you."

"Get out of here," Blade commanded.

Mousy turned and started from the alley. He paused next to Skinny. "What about my buddy?"

"Take him with you," Blade said.

Geronimo looked at Blade. "Awwww, gee! I was hoping I could split his head open. Can I? Huh? Can I? Pretty please?"

Blade barely supressed a laugh. "No."

"Darn!" Geronimo exclaimed wistfully.

Mousy gawked at Geronimo. "You're wacko, Indian!

All of you are flat-out crazy!"

Geronimo beamed. "You really think so?"

Mousy and Skinny moved toward the alley entrance.

Hickok suddenly blocked their path, the Henry in his hands. He aimed the barrel at Mousey's face. "Hold it!"

"What's the matter?" Mousy queried nervously. "The guy with the knife said we could go."

"Is that a wart on your nose?" Hickok asked.

"A what?"

"A wart," Hickok reiterated. "I'm not partial to warts. I plug 'em every chance I get. If that's a wart on your nose, I'll have to shoot it off."

Mousy gazed back at Blade and Geronimo, then stared at Helen for a second. "Lunatics! I'm surrounded by lunatics!"

"Is that a wart?" Hickok repeated.

"There's no damn wart on my nose!" Mousy said anxiously.

"Oh." Hickok lowered the Henry. "In that case, have a real nice day." He bowed and motioned toward the main street.

Mousy grabbed Skinny's right arm. "Come on! We're getting the hell out of here!"

The two mobsters ran from the alley and disappeared.

Helen began laughing.

Blade and Geronimo joined their colleagues.

"Were you serious about going after Don Giorgio?" Hickok asked.

Blade replaced the right Bowie in its sheath. "Of course not. I wanted to buy us time to find Mindy. If Giorgio expects us at his Palace, he might drop the tails. We should have a few hours before he gets suspicious."

Hickok chuckled. "By the time the cow chip realizes we're not comin', we'll be long gone with Mindy."

"I hope," Blade said.

Geronimo slid the tomahawk under his belt. "So now we find Mindy," he remarked with determination.

"About time," Helen muttered.

Hickok looked up and noticed Blade was thoughtfully

chewing on his lower lip. "What's buggin' you?"

"Something is not right," Blade said.

"Like what?" Hickok questioned.

Blade frowned. "I don't know. I can't put my finger on it. There's something I'm missing."

"It'll come to you," Hickok said. "Give it time."

"I guess you're right," Blade argued. He stared at Helen. "Let's go rescue your daughter."

"And keep your eyes peeled," Hickok told Helen.

Helen gazed at the gunman quizzically. "For what?"

"Mobsters with warts. I can use some target practice," Hickok commented.

Helen simply rolled her eyes heavenward.

CHAPTER NINE

"What's that, pard?" Hickok asked.

The four Warriors stood near an intersection over a half mile from the alley.

Blade flipped through the pages of the small black book he'd removed from his right rear pocket. "I found this on the body of the stranger killed at the scene of Mindy's abduction. I'm double-checking the address for the Golden Crown Casino. That's where Pucci told Ted we'd find Mindy. And the mobster in the alley confirmed the Golden Crown Casino is Pucci's personal casino."

"We never did figure out why the stranger was killed," Geronimo mentioned.

"Maybe Pucci will tell us," Hickok said.

Blade found the address he wanted, then closed the black book and returned it to his rear pocket, slipping the book alongside the wad of two thousand dollars and the piece of blue plastic. "This is the correct boulevard. The Golden Crown Casino should be just up ahead."

Helen hefted her Carbine. "I pray she's all right."

"She will be," Hickok assured her.

"Let's go," Blade declared.

The quartet crossed the intersection.

"Any sign of a tail?" Blade inquired.

Geronimo, bringing up the rear, shook his head. "Nope. Don Giorgio must be waiting for us at his casino."

Blade scrutinized the buildings ahead as he sauntered along the sidewalk. They passed several casinos, liquor stores, one food store, and a gas station crammed with cars. He stared at the pumps, puzzled. Where did the mobsters obtain their fuel? Gasoline was a precious commodity elsewhere; the Civilized Zone and California stringently accounted for every gallon. Las Vegas, though, possessed gas in abundance. He gazed up at a flickering neon sign. There was another rarity: electrical power. The Outlands were totally devoid of such a luxury, and even California and the Civilized Zone, where generating plants were scrupulously maintained, were forced to conserve their useage, primarily supplying power to the urban centers.

The mobsters, though, were under no such limitations.

How did they do it?

Blade walked ten more yards and happened to glance at a casino sign fifty yards distant.

THE GOLDEN CROWN CASINO.

"Blade," Geronimo said, his alert eyes having already spied the sign.

"I see it," Blade stated, halting.

"See what?" Helen inquired.

Blade pointed toward the sign.

Helen took one look and started to head for it.

"Hold it," Blade directed, gripping her right wrist.

Helen angrily attempted to pull free. "Let me go! Mindy is in there!"

"We need a plan," Blade said.

"Plan, hell! I want to go to Mindy!" Helen snapped.

"Calm down!" Blade instructed her.

Helen's lips tightened, but she relaxed her arm. "Okay. What do we do?"

"We can't all go in at once," Blade said. "Pucci would

spot us too easily."

"Do you suppose he has our descriptions?" Geronimo asked.

"Could be," Blade said. "Remember, he asked for me by name. He must have some idea of how I look."

"Yeah," Hickok quipped. "It isn't every day you run into a seven-foot giant with big ears."

"His ears are no bigger than your mouth," Geronimo cracked.

"We'll go in two at a time," Blade proposed. "Geronimo and I will go in first. Hickok, give us three minutes and come in with Helen."

"I want to go in with you," Helen said to Blade.

"No."

"Why not?" Helen questioned in annoyance.

"Because I know you," Blade said. "If you spot Mindy in there, you'll start shooting every mobster in sight. I'm going in first to see if she's there."

"I'll watch over Helen," Hickok promised.

Blade inspected the Commando, insuring the safety was off. "Then let's get to it."

"Not so fast," Geronimo cautioned. "We have a problem."

"What kind of problem?" Blade asked.

Geronimo nodded at the opposite sidewalk. "See for yourself."

Blade turned, surveying the far sidewalk, perplexed until he recognized two faces in the seething crowd. "Damn!" he exclaimed.

Mousy and two other mobsters were standing on the opposite walk, and Mousy was gesturing at the Warriors and talking rapidly.

"Where'd he come from?" Hickok queried. "How'd he get here so fast?"

"He had a car, remember?" Blade reminded the gunman.

Mousy and his two companions unexpectedly began running, rudely shoving pedestrians aside, heading in the same direction as the Warriors.

"What's that all about?" Helen wanted to know.

Blade studied the casinos on the far side of the boulevard. Fifty yards away was the answer, a casino with its name in bright red letters overhead.

JOHNNY'S PALACE.

Mousy and the two mobsters were heading for the Palace as swiftly as the logjam of pedestrians permitted.

"Johnny's Palace," Geronimo said. "It's right across the street from the Golden Crown Casino!"

Blade stared from the Palace to the Golden Crown, feeling frustrated. He'd never expected this! Why were Don Giorgio's Palace and Don Pucci's Casino directly across the boulevard from one another? Was the territory on the far side of the boulevard Giorgio's? Was this side Pucci's?

"We can still find Mindy," Helen declared. "This doesn't change a thing."

"Yes, it does," Blade said, disputing her. "If we go into the Golden Crown and rescue Mindy, we'll undoubtedly have to take on Don Pucci's men to free her. And when we come out, Don Giorgio's men will be waiting for us. I don't like the odds."

"We could leave," Geronimo suggested, "then try and get inside the Golden Crown after dark. Maybe we won't be spotted by Giorgio's hit men."

"I'm not leaving!" Helen vowed.

"I have a plan," Hickok mentioned softly.

"Even if we do leave," Blade said, ignoring the gunman, "there's no guarantee we can sneak into the Golden Crown undetected after nightfall. Look at all those neon lights. This whole city must be lit up like one of those ancient Christmas trees."

"I have a plan," Hickok repeated quietly.

"Then let's march into the Golden Crown, and hang the consequences!" Geronimo advocated.

"I have a plan," Hickok said.

Blade sighed and faced the gunman. "I know I'll regret

this, but what's your plan?"

"It'll be a piece of cake," Hickok assured them. "We need to keep Don Giorgio occupied while we're savin' Mindy. So one of us should go into the Palace to keep Giorgio busy while the rest go into the Golden Crown and find Mindy."

"I'm surprised," Geronimo remarked. "He has a good plan."

Blade ran his left hand through his hair. Hickok's idea did make sense. With Giorgio preoccupied, three Warriors should be more than enough to quickly effect Mindy's release. "It might work," he grudgingly conceded.

"Then I reckon I'll see you yahoos later," Hickok said, and took a step toward the curb.

"Hold it," Blade said. "I'll go to the Palace."

"Don't be a donkey," Hickok objected. "You're the brains of this outfit. If anyone can figure a way to get Mindy out of the Golden Crown, it's you. Helen should go with you because she's Mindy's mom. And Geronimo has to go with you too, because he can't hoodwink folks the way I can."

"I can hoodwink as good as you any day!" Geronimo responded, then paused. "What's hoodwink mean, anyway?"

Hickok stared into Blade's eyes. "You can see I'm right, can't you?"

Blade reluctantly nodded. "You go."

"Why am I so blamed brilliant all the time?" Hickok mumbled, and stepped to the curb.

"Wait!" Blade declared. "Cross at the next intersection!"

Hickok looked at each of them. "The direct approach, remember?" He winked at Geronimo. "Take care of that mangy, low-down, lyin' Injun butt of yours."

Geronimo started to reply, but the gunman was gone.

Hickok darted into the traffic, swinging his Henry from side to side, weaving between the cars. Some of the drivers slammed on their brakes at the sight of the Warrior. Others ducked for cover when the Henry swung in their direction. There was a lot of metallic squealing and grinding intermixed with curses and screams, but the gunfighter reached the opposite side of the boulevard unscathed.

Geronimo expelled a deep breath. "I wish he wouldn't pull stunts like that."

"If he didn't," Blade commented, "he wouldn't be Hickok."

"Too bad he's married," Helen remarked.

"Hickok will give us the time we need," Blade said, heading for the Golden Crown. "Let's make sure his sacrifice is not in vain."

"Sacrifice?" Helen repeated. "You sound like you don't expect to see him again."

Blade watched the gunman wade through the stream of pedestrians on the far walk. "We may not," he said grimly, then stalked toward the Golden Crown Casino.

Don Anthony Pucci's personal casino was an imposing, stately structure 15 stories in height. Ten glass doors faced the boulevard, each with its frame painted a metallic gold. The trim on the windows was also gold. While the exterior on the upper floors was an opaque black glass, the lowest floor was a clean, white stucco. Patrons were flocking in and out of the casino constantly.

Blade walked up the three cement steps to the first door and gripped the handle. He paused long enough to glance across the boulevard at Johnny's Palace.

Hickok was just entering Giorgio's casino.

Blade opened the door and stepped inside, the Commando in his right hand.

Geronimo and Helen followed.

Blade walked several yards and stopped to get his bearings.

The lobby of the Golden Crown was opulently, tastefully furnished with plush red carpet, subdued blue walls decorated with paintings, and chandeliers to provide the illumination. Customers were everywhere.

Geronimo tapped Blade on the left arm and pointed at a sign on the nearby wall.

WELCOME!

The Golden Crown management welcomes you to the ultimate gambling experience! Exchange Centers are located throughout the casino. If you have any questions, our helpful Hostesses will gladly assist you. Enforcers are on the premises at all times to discourage disorderly behavior. The first drink is on the house. Thank you and come again!

Blade surveyed the enormous lobby, scanning the hundreds of people engaged in a variety of activities; some were seated at tables, playing cards; some were seated around a large wheel; others were at tables where cards were pulled from wooden boxes; and over two hundred were yanking levers on odd machines with flashing lights and twirling fruit emblems.

"How will we ever find Mindy in here?" Geronimo wondered aloud.

A petite brunette in a red and black outfit, her red, ruffled skirt barely covering her thighs, approached the Warriors with a wide smile. A square blue plastic tag attached to her black blouse identified her as a HOSTESS.

"Hello," she greeted them. "My name is Leslie. Welcome to the Golden Crown."

"Hello," Blade said.

Leslie raked them with a critical eye. "My! You certainly are armed to the teeth! Expecting trouble?"

"You can't be too careful these days," Blade commented.

"May I help you in any way?" Leslie asked.

"We're looking for someone," Blade told her. "A young woman named Mindy."

"Is she an employee of the Golden Crown?" Leslie asked.

"We know she was brought here," Blade replied. "I don't think she would be an employee."

"Is she a guest?" Leslie inquired politely.

"She's my daughter," Helen interjected brusquely.

"I can check the casino register to see if she's a guest,"

Leslie offered. "What's her last name?"

"She doesn't have one," Helen said.

Leslie grinned. "Everyone has a last name."

Helen leaned toward the hostess, her eyes flinty. "We don't. Neither does Mindy. We know she's here. Tell Don Pucci we want her!"

The hostess blinked twice. "Don Pucci?"

"Yes," Blade stated courteously. "We're here at Don Pucci's invitation. Tell him the Warriors have arrived."

"The Warriors?" Leslie repeated quizzically.

"Do it!" Helen snapped impatiently.

Leslie's eyes widened slightly. "I'll be right back," she promised, and walked off to the left.

"Why'd you give us away?" Geronimo asked Blade.

"I didn't," Blade said, glancing at Helen. "Blabbermouth here did."

"I'm sorry," Helen said, not sounding sorry at all. "I'm tired of pussyfooting around! It's obvious we could search for weeks in a building this huge and never find Mindy. So I decided to try Hickok's method, the direct approach."

"Now we're in trouble," Geronimo said.

"Why?" Helen queried.

Geronimo gazed around the casino. "Because Hickok's method only works for Hickok. I call it the Blundering Idiot Principle."

"The harm is done," Blade stated. "We'll have to play it by ear from here on out and pray for the best."

"I'd like it better if Pucci didn't know we're here," Geronimo observed.

Blade cradled the Commando in his arms. The colossal casino would be impossible to search completely from top to bottom, so Helen's blunder was logically justified. But he was peeved at her for taking the initiative without his approval. He intended to submit her to a refresher course in the necessity for Warrior obedience after they returned to the Home.

If they returned.

"Here comes the bimbo," Helen declared.

The hostess walked up to them, smiling sweetly. "I

called the main office. They're sending someone down to see you."

"Thanks," Blade said.

"Mind if I ask you a question?" Geronimo mentioned.

"That's what I'm here for," Leslie responded.

"This is our first trip to Vegas," Geronimo revealed. "And there are some things I don't understand. For instance, why do the casinos accept prewar currency? Without the Government of the United States to back the money, isn't it worthless?"

"Prewar currency is not worthless because it's backed by the casinos," Leslie said. "Let me explain. I asked about this once, and this is what my supervisor told me. There is a lot of prewar currency floating around. Its face value is zero, but the Dons decided to use the prewar currency instead of printing their own money. All of the national mints stopped functioning during the war. No one has the capability to make money. So the Dons use the existing currency at an exchange rate of pennies on the dollar. It's cheaper for them than manufacturing their own."

"But eventually all the prewar currency will wear out," Geronimo noted. "What will they do then?"

"I don't know," Leslie said. "But they have a process for partially restoring really old bills. It will be a long time before all the prewar currency is gone."

"I have a question," Blade remarked. "How is it Las Vegas has so much gas and unlimited electricity?"

"You can get anything on the black market if you have the price," Leslie said enigmatically.

"Are you married?" Helen unexpectedly inquired.

"Yes, I am," Leslie answered. "Why?"

"How can you live in Las Vegas, you being a married woman and all?" Helen questioned.

"I don't understand," Leslie said.

"Look around you! All this gambling. Gangsters all over the place. Shootings on the streets," Helen detailed. "How can you live in such an environment?"

"What's wrong with Vegas?" Leslie responded. "Life here is good. We never have shortages of food, or clothing, or gas. The Dons protect the city from the looters and the mutants. And if you don't carry a gun, odds are you'll never be involved in a shooting. The standard of living in Vegas is higher than in most other parts of the country. The schools are excellent—"

"You have schools?" Blade interrupted.

"Of course, silly," Leslie said. "How else would we educate our children? The Dons funnel a large portion of their profits into the educational system."

"The Dons support the schools?" Blade asked in surprise.

"And the hospitals, and the utilities, and the senior centers," Leslie divulged. "Didn't you know that?"

"No," Blade confessed, "I had no idea."

"The Dons care about their people," Leslie stated affectionately.

"Will wonders never cease!" Geronimo quipped.

A lean man with black hair, a square jaw, and glasses, attired in a white suit, was walking toward the Warriors with a hurried tread. He smiled as he neared them. "Hello. My name is Mario Pileggi. I'm Don Pucci's Operations Manager." He extended his right hand to Blade.

Blade took the hand and shook, Pileggi's firm handshake and clear blue eyes disconcerting him. "I'm Blade. This is Helen and Geronimo." He perceived that Pileggi was an urbane, confident man.

"I was told you want to see Don Pucci?" Mario said when Blade released his hand.

"We're here at his invitation," Blade stated.

Mario studied the three Warriors for a few seconds. "This is most mystifying. Perhaps you would be kind enough to accompany me to the main office. We can sort this out there."

"What's to sort out?" Helen demanded. "I want my daughter."

"Where is your daughter?" Mario asked.

"Don't play games! You know she's here. The Don took her!" Helen said angrily.

"Hmmmm," was all Mario replied.

"We would like to get this sorted out as quickly as possible," Blade commented.

"Come with me," Mario said, and turned and headed for the far side of the lobby.

Blade kept his finger on the trigger of the Commando as he crossed the spacious floor. If Mario was leading them into a trap, he wanted to be ready. They passed a row of those odd machines with the lights and rotating pictures of fruit. "What are those?" he inquired.

Mario glanced over his right shoulder, his forehead creased. "You've never seen a slot machine before?"

"No," Blade said.

Mario halted and reached into his left front pants pocket. He withdrew a circular red plastic piece and handed it to the giant.

Blade took the piece. There was lettering on both sides. THE GOLDEN CROWN.

"It's a token," Mario mentioned. "There's a chronic shortage of coins, so we use tokens in some of the slots. This one's on the house."

"Thank you," Blade said, pocketing the token, puzzled.

Mario continued toward the far wall.

Blade was feeling uncharacteristically tense. Something was gnawing at his mind, troubling him. What *was* it? Why was he so certain he was overlooking an important factor in this mission?

A glass-enclosed elevator appeared through the crowd. Mario was heading straight for it.

Blade surveyed the patrons for any sign of Enforcers or button men, but none were in evidence.

Mario indicated the elevator when they were ten feet away. "We'll take this up to the second floor."

"Is Don Pucci's office on the second floor?" Blade queried.

"The main office is on the second floor," Mario replied.

The elevator was large enough to accommodate a dozen occupants. A sign was affixed to the glass in the middle. RESERVED. RESTRICTED USE. Two glass doors comprised the front of the elevator.

"The public elevators are over there," Mario said, pointing at four elevators 20 yards to the left.

"I was surprised to find this casino so close to Don Giorgio's," Blade absently commented.

Mario, about to reach for the gold handles in the center of the glass doors, froze and turned. "You know Don Giorgio?"

"No," Blade said.

Mario's mouth curled downwards. "Giorgio is an upstart. He deliberately built his casino across from Don Pucci's."

"Why?" Blade asked. "To increase his business?"

"Not hardly," Mario answered. "He had ulterior motives." He opened the elevator doors. "After you."

"After you," Blade said.

Mario shrugged and entered the elevator, standing next to a panel of buttons.

The Warriors stepped into the elevator.

Mario closed the doors and pushed a button marked with a 2. The elevator started upward.

"Are Don Pucci and Don Giorgio friends?" Blade questioned.

Mario laughed bitterly. "Friends isn't the word I would use."

The elevator coasted to a stop on the second floor. Below, the lobby was a jumble of bustling movement.

Mario turned. The rear of the elevator was a seemingly solid black plastic wall. He pressed a black button on the panel and the "wall" slid into a recessed slot on the right, revealing a lengthy corridor beyond.

Blade realized the glass portion only faced the lobby. Access to the corridors was through this rear door.

"Allow me," Mario said, taking the lead and exiting. He took an abrupt right.

Blade, Geronimo, and Helen stepped from the elevator.

Mario had stopped and was facing them, grinning triumphantly. The rear door to the elevator hissed shut. "Would you care to tell me the real reason you want to see the Don?"

"We've already told you," Helen responded testily. "I want my daughter."

Mario sighed and raised his right hand. "I was hoping you would cooperate." He snapped his fingers.

Doors all along the corridor suddenly opened, disgorging over a dozen somber men in suits, each armed with a machine gun. They trained their weapons on the Warriors.

"If you make a move," Mario warned in a pleasant tone, "you're dead."

CHAPTER TEN

Hickok strolled into Johnny's Palace with the Henry slung over his back and his thumbs hooked in his gunbelt. He paused just inside one of the seven glass doors, studying the layout.

Johnny's Palace was ornate, garishly decorated with an ostentatious green carpet and gaudy orange and yellow walls. Oversized chandeliers hung from the arched ceiling. The gambling was in full swing and customers crammed the joint.

A pretty blonde in a transparent, skimpy yellow dress walked up to the gunman.

"Hi there, handsome," she declared, smiling broadly. "Looking for a good time?"

Hickok noticed an orange tag imprinted with the word ESCORT pinned below her left shoulder. "Howdy, ma'am," he replied. "I'm lookin' for Don Giorgio."

The escort lost her smile. "Why do you want to see him?"

"That's personal," Hickok said.

"No one can see Don Giorgio without an appointment,"

the escort stated.

"Where would I find him?" Hickok asked.

"Didn't you hear me?" the escort responded. "You can't see him without an appointment."

Hickok lowered his voice. "Ma'am, if you don't spill the beans, right this moment, I'm afraid I'll be obliged to shoot you in the foot."

The escort did a double take. "You wouldn't dare!"

Hickok's mouth creased in a lopsided grin. "Try me."

She scrutinized him from head to toe, then stared into his blue eyes for a moment. "I just bet you'd do it too!"

"Where can I find Giorgio?" Hickok queried again.

"You're making a big mistake, mister," the escort said.

"I make 'em all the time," Hickok noted. "So what's one more? Now where is Giorgio?"

The escort turned and pointed at a wall on the opposite side of the lobby. "Do you see those doors there?"

Hickok looked. There were three wooden doors spaced about 20 yards apart visible through the crowd. "Yep."

"The middle door is Don Giorgio's office," she said.

"Is that a fact?" Hickok commented. "You wouldn't lie to me, would you?"

Her cheeks reddened. "Don't you believe me?"

"Nope," Hickok stated. "The Don isn't likely to have his office right out in the open, where anyone can mosey in anytime they feel like it. I'd imagine the Don is one cautious hombre. So where is his real office?"

The escort frowned. "Third floor. He has a suite at the end of the hall. The elevators and the stairs are to the left of those doors."

Hickok reached up and patted her on the left cheek. "Thank you, ma'am. That wasn't so hard, was it?"

"If the Don discovers I told you," she said fearfully, "he'll kill me!"

"Don't you worry," Hickok assured her. "He'll never know." He motioned at the wall to his right. "I want you to stand right there, where I can keep an eye on you, until I get across the lobby. You might be tempted to warn the Don, and I can't let you do that."

The escort walked over to the wall and stood there meekly.

"Thanks again," Hickok said cheerfully, and started toward the far side of the room. He scanned the packed patrons, noting the various games they were playing.

Out of the corner of his right eye, Hickok saw the blonde escort edging toward a wooden door 15 feet from the front entrance. He grinned, but otherwise pretended not to notice. Another minute or so and he'd have the welcoming committee he wanted.

The throng of spectators and gamblers shifted, and Hickok caught sight of three men in suits, men with countenances hardened like granite. None held weapons, but their jackets were open and each man had one hand near his waist.

"Excuse me!" a voice commanded, and Mousy appeared, shoving his way through the spectators.

Hickok grinned. "Well, if it isn't Wart-Nose," he addressed the diminutive mobster. "Long time no see!"

Mousy's beady eyes narrowed. "Don't call me Wart-Nose!"

"How about Poop-for-Brains?" Hickok quipped.

"Funny man!" Mousy snapped. "But you made the biggest mistake of your life when you waltzed into here!"

"I didn't waltz," Hickok corrected him. "I walked."

"Did you really think Don Giorgio would see you?" Mousy demanded.

"It'd be the smart thing to do," Hickok remarked.

"What do you know about smarts?" Mousy declared. "You're so dumb, it's pathetic."

"Are you going to take me to Don Giorgio?" Hickok inquired.

"Dream on!" Mousy said.

"He doesn't want to talk to me?"

Mousy snorted. "He wants to snuff you, jerk! You and all of your friends are to blame for his son's death!"

"You've got it all wrong, Wart-Nose," Hickok baited the button man.

"No, I don't!" Mousy snapped. "The big geek with the

knives told me that you guys whacked Franky!"

Hickok shook his head. "They didn't. I did."

"You killed Franky?" Mousy queried, astounded the gunman would bluntly confess.

"Yep," Hickok said. "I was the one who plugged Franky. My pards shot Franky's cronies."

Mousy glanced at his chums. "Did you hear this jerk?"

"Enough small talk," Hickok stated. "I want you to take me to Giorgio. Now."

Mousy snickered. "No way."

"Take me or die," Hickok said softly.

The spectators abruptly wanted to be somewhere else. They scrambled to put as much distance as possible between themselves and the imminent violence. All except for an elderly woman, who kept avidly sticking coins into her purse.

"Do you really think you can take on all four of us by yourself?" Mousy asked sarcastically.

"If you try and draw on me," Hickok responded, "none of you will live long enough to touch your guns."

"You smug asshole!" Mousy declared. "You're history!" He grabbed for the pistol in a concealed holster on his right hip.

The other three mobsters also went for their guns. All three were experienced Enforcers, experts at their lethal craft. Each one considered himself fast and accurate. Each one had outdrawn opponents at one time or another. But not one had ever beheld the spectacular speed of the gunfighter in buckskins.

One moment Hickok's hands were draped at his sides. The next, in a literal blur of consummate swiftness, the Pythons were out and leveled and blasting.

Mousy was hit high on the forehead by both slugs, the brutal impact catapulting him backwards into a blackjack table. He crashed onto his back, his arms outspread.

Hickok swiveled to cover the remaining three hit men. They were imitating trees, frozen in place with their limbs at odd angles, having turned to ice in the process of reaching for their weapons. Not one had managed to move their gun hand more than an inch. "What's it going to be, gents?" Hickok asked. "Do you want to die?"

Each one shook his head.

"Then unlimber your hardware, real easy like," Hickok instructed them. "One wrong twitch and I'll perforate your noggins."

The mobsters carefully eased their handguns from their holsters and ever-so-slowly set the guns on the floor.

"Now back up three steps," Hickok directed.

They obeyed.

Hickok heard a door slam and glanced at the far wall. A dozen mobsters were coming toward him, led by a tall man with a cleft chin, a beaked nose, dark eyes, and white hair, and wearing a gray suit. Many of the mobsters carried machine guns, and Hickok girded himself for a battle royal. He grinned, hoping he would acquit himself with honor.

"Don't shoot!" the man with the white hair shouted. "Don't shoot! We want to talk!"

The mobsters were over 40 yards off, but still advancing.

"That's close enough!" Hickok called out.

The man with the white hair said something to his henchmen and they halted.

"What do we have to talk about?" Hickok yelled.

"We don't want any more shooting!" the man with the white hair said. "Can I come closer?"

"Come ahead," Hickok replied.

The man with the white hair cautiously came toward the Warrior. He stared at Mousy's corpse for several seconds, then at the patrons ringing the lobby. "My name is Kenney," he said when he was within speaking range.

"You're Giorgio's right-hand man?" Hickok queried, recalling the comments Mousy made in the alley earlier.

Kenney nodded. He stopped, scrutinizing the gunfighter. "Who are you?"

"The handle is . . ." Hickok began, and paused. What name should he give? Blade had given a false name to that Enforcer because the Big Guy didn't want Don Pucci to know the Warriors were in Las Vegas. Should he do the same? If he gave his real name, would Pucci find out? Did it even matter, since Blade and the others were in the Golden Crown rescuing Mindy? Maybe he should play it safe. "Earp. Wyatt Earp."

Kenney's eyes narrowed and his forehead creased. "Mr. Earp, my boss would like to talk to you."

"Don Giorgio wants to see me?" Hickok responded skeptically.

"Yes. He sent me down to invite you up to his suite," Kenney said. "He's been watching you since Security reported you were here."

"He has?" Hickok queried.

"Yes," Kenney confirmed. "The whole casino is under constant surveillance by hidden cameras."

"Why does Giorgio want to see me?" Hickok questioned.

"You must ask him," Kenney replied. "Will you come with me?"

Hickok nodded toward the other mobsters. "What about those cow chips?"

"They'll stay down here, if such is your wish," Kenney said.

"It'd make me feel a mite more relaxed," Hickok remarked. "My trigger fingers can become awful itchy."

"You won't need your guns," Kenney commented. "No harm will come to you."

"No one is takin' my Colts," Hickok vowed.

"I simply meant you don't need to keep your revolvers in your hands," Kenney elaborated. "You can put them in your holsters."

"They'll stay right where they are," Hickok said. "You lead the way. And whatever you do, don't trip. I might accidentally blow your spine out your bellybutton."

Kenney turned and walked toward the far wall. "There won't be any trouble," he said over his left shoulder.

"For your sake, I hope not," Hickok stated. He constantly shifted his gaze from gangster to gangster, ready to gun down the first one who made a hostile move. But they and stood still, eyeing him contemptuously. What was

Giorgio up to? he wondered. Giorgio didn't sound like the forgiving sort. So why did Giorgio want to palaver all of a sudden?

And why, Hickok asked himself, did he have the feeling he was going from the frying pan into the fire?

CHAPTER ELEVEN

Blade could feel his stomach muscles tightening into a compact knot as he stared at the machine guns trained on Helen, Geronimo, and himself.

"Drop your weapons!" Mario commanded.

"Never!" Helen snapped. "Hand over my daughter!"

Mario adjusted his glasses on his nose. He gazed at the giant and spoke calmly. "I don't want any needless bloodshed."

"Neither do we," Blade assured him.

"Then drop your weapons," Mario directed. "You'll be cut down if you try to resist."

Blade glanced at the man in the white suit, gauging the distance between them as four feet. "You won't shoot if we put our weapons on the floor?" he asked.

"No. You have my personal guarantee," Mario stated.

"Okay," Blade said meekly. "We'll do it."

"I won't!" Helen objected. "No one is taking my weapons!"

Blade looked at her. "You'll do exactly as I say!" he ordered. "After I put my Commando down, you do the same with your carbine." He deliberately accented the word "after."

Helen frowned. "If you insist!"

Blade gazed at Geronimo. "Do you understand?"

Geronimo nodded. "I understand perfectly."

Blade faced the man in white. "Here goes. Tell your men not to shoot."

"They won't fire unless I give the signal," Mario disclosed.

Blade nodded. "I was hoping you would say that." He bent over at the waist and deposited his Commando on the red carpet. Releasing the gun, he started to straighten, and as he did he made his move. His right hand whipped his corresponding Bowie free of its sheath, even as he bounded toward Mario, covering the four feet in an easy, quick stride. Before the mobsters in the corridor could fire, he had his left arm around Mario's shoulders and the right Bowie pressed against the gangster's neck.

Several of the button men had swiveled, trying to bring their machine guns to bear on the giant, but he had moved too swiftly and was too close to Mario Pileggi to permit them to fire.

"Freeze!" Blade barked, using Mario's body as a shield. "If just one of you tries anything, this man is dead!"

Mario appeared stunned by the unexpected reversal. "Don't shoot!" he shouted at his men. "Do as he says!"

"I want all of your guns on the floor! Now!" Blade instructed them.

The hit men hesitated, collectively focused on Mario.

"Do it!" Mario yelled. "Now!"

Hesitantly, the mobsters slowly lowered their machine guns to the floor.

"Now put your hands up and step away from your guns!" Blade declared.

"Do it!" Mario added.

The button men moved back.

Geronimo hastily retrieved Blade's Commando while keeping his Browning BAR trained on their foes.

Blade dug the tip of the Bowie into Mario's sweating

neck. "Now I want to see Don Pucci."

"Never!" Mario said.

"Let me have him!" Helen interjected, incensed. "I'll make him take us to Pucci!"

"Never!" Mario reiterated. "None of us will betray our Don!"

"How touching!" Helen said sarcastically. "He's being loyal to the bastard who kidnapped my daughter!"

Mario's eyes narrowed as he intently studied Helen. "You're serious!" he exclaimed.

Helen took a menacing stride toward him. "Of course I'm serious, you dimwit! What have I been telling you! The Don abducted Mindy, and I want her back now!"

Mario tried to twist his head so he could see the giant holding him, but the sharp point of the Bowie prevented him from turning. "You can release me," he said.

"Not on your life," Blade stated. "You're our ticket out of here, our insurance against interference."

"If you want to see Don Pucci, you'd better let me go," Mario advised. "I promise you I'll arrange a meeting."

"Why should we trust you?" Blade demanded.

"Because I believe your story," Mario said. "I believe this woman's daughter was abducted, and I believe you think Don Pucci is responsible. I didn't believe her before. I thought you were using the story as a ruse to get close to the Don so you could whack him."

"If he took my daughter," Helen remarked bitterly, "he's as good as dead!"

Blade glanced at Geronimo. "Cover us. I'm going to release him."

Geronimo nodded, scrutinizing the hit men.

Blade eased his Bowie away from Mario's neck and straightened. "There. Now let's see if your word is worth anything."

Mario gingerly rubbed his sore neck with his right hand, and when he withdrew his hand there was a trickle of blood on his fingers. "That's some knife you've got there," he mentioned.

Blade wiped the Bowie on his pants leg. "I'm fond of it."

"I'll escort you down to the casino," Mario said. "You can wait there until Don Pucci comes down. And don't worry. We're not about to attack you in our own casino. Business would suffer."

"What do you mean?" Blade asked.

"The casino is our drawing card, so to speak," Mario elaborated. "Our rooms on the upper floors are always filled to capacity because our customers know they can gamble here in safety. They know Don Pucci runs an honest house, unlike some of the other Dons. Whenever you have a shooting in a casino, business suffers. The customers shy away for a while. We don't want that."

Blade walked over to Geronimo and took the Commando. "We'll wait for Don Pucci, and you have my word that we won't start shooting unless you start something."

"We won't," Mario assured the giant. He moved to the wall and pressed a red button, then looked at Helen. "I'm sorry I didn't believe you. But you must understand my position. There are a lot of people who would like to see Don Pucci dead, and I would give my life to protect him. So would everyone else in his Family."

"Why did Don Pucci kidnap my daughter?" Helen asked bluntly.

"He didn't," Mario replied.

"I know better," Helen stated.

"You can talk to the Don in person," Mario said. "Then let's see how you feel."

The inner door to the elevator slid open as the elevator arrived on the second floor.

Mario entered.

The Warriors backed into the elevator, their weapons aimed at the mobsters in the corridor.

Blade breathed a slight sigh of relief when the door slid shut. He gazed down at the throngs of gamblers as the elevator descended, spying a long bar on the south side of the enormous room. Anyone approaching the bar from the gaming tables and the slot machines would need to cover 20 yards of open space. The bar was an ideal spot to await the Don.

With a scarcely perceptible jolt, the elevator stopped.

Mario exited first, standing to the right of the open doors.

"We'll be waiting at the bar," Blade said as he emerged.

"Give me ten minutes," Mario said.

"Five," Blade amended as Geronimo and Helen joined him.

Mario shook his head. "I need ten. You'll understand the reason when you see the Don."

"Ten, then," Blade said. "But one minute longer and we'll tear your casino apart."

Mario stepped into the elevator, closed the doors, and nodded at the Warriors as it climbed.

"I don't trust him!" Helen opined. "Why did you agree to this nonsense?"

"Sometimes a Warrior must rely on his or her intuition," Blade answered. "My intuition tells me to trust Mario this time."

"I pray you're right," Helen said. She scanned the patrons at the nearby tables, her features downcast. "All I want is to find Mindy and return safely to the Home. Is that too much to ask?"

"No," Blade stated. He headed in the direction of the bar, alert for an assault.

"If it's any consolation," Geronimo commented, staying abreast of Blade on the right, "I agree with you."

The Warriors skirted the gaming tables and the slot machines, winding toward the south side of the casino. The laughter, the tinkle of glasses filled with liquor, and the smiling customers were an odd contrast to the deadly mobsters running the establishment. Blade observed the patrons heartily enjoying themselves, and he remembered the words of the woman at the diner. The Organized Crime Families had controlled Las Vegas for over a century, and the citizens and tourists all seemed content with the status quo. Why? How could they allow their lives to be run by the Dons? Was it because life under the Dons was better, in a materialistic sense, than life elsewhere in the country? Was it because the Dons were no more oppressive than the government which they had supplanted? Or was it because the Dons and Las Vegas were made for each other? They both flourished in an atmosphere of permissiveness and they naturally attracted others of a similar persuasion.

The bar appeared ahead.

Blade ceased his reflection and walked up to the middle of the bar.

"I wonder how Hickok is doing," Geronimo commented.

"As soon as we finish our business here," Blade said, "we'll go get him."

"If anything happens to him," Geronimo pledged, "I won't leave Las Vegas until I settle accounts with Don Giorgio."

"Look!" Helen declared. "The elevator."

The glass elevator was descending.

"Here they come!" Helen said excitedly. "Now we'll learn where Mindy is!"

A party of men left the elevator and moved through the customers, coming toward the Warriors.

Blade's superior height enabled him to see the party clearly, and his forehead furrowed in confusion when he spotted the head of the group.

"Don Pucci better turn Mindy over to us!" Helen was saying.

Blade stared at the floor, deep in thought.

"What is it?" Geronimo inquired.

"You'll see in a moment," Blade responded.

The party of mobsters came even closer. There were ten men, eight of whom were armed with machine guns. The ninth was Mario. And the tenth was a man with gray hair, a man with a thin face and a pale complexion, a man in a beige suit with a red blanket covering his lap because he was seated in a wheelchair!

"What the hell is this?" Helen snapped.

The eight men with machine guns fanned out around

Mario and the man in the wheelchair, forming a protective semicircle.

Mario pushed the wheelchair up to the Warriors. "Allow me the honor of introducing Don Anthony Pucci."

"Hello," Blade said.

"This is the Don?" Helen inquired in shocked disbelief.

Don Pucci's piercing blue eyes belied his physical condition. He critically inspected each of the Warriors, then focused on Blade. "Mario has been telling me about you," he stated in a deep, vibrant voice. "I don't often leave my private quarters anymore, but I decided to make an exception in your case." He looked at Helen. "What is this bull about my kidnapping your daughter?"

Helen was completely confounded. "You can't be the Don!" she blurted out.

Don Pucci grinned. "I assure you I am. Ask anyone." He caught sight of one of the bartenders behind the bar, busily tending to a customer. "Hey! Arthur!"

The bartender glanced up, saw the man in the wheelchair, and instantly hastened down the bar. "Yes, sir! What would you like?"

"Arthur, would you tell this woman who I am?" Don Pucci requested.

Arthur gazed at Helen. "He's Don Pucci. Everybody knows that."

"Thank you, Arthur," the Don said. "How's the family?"

Arthur, a hefty man with a mustache, smiled. "They're fine, sir. Bobby has a birthday in a week. He'll be ten."

"Expect a little gift for him," Don Pucci stated.

Arthur beamed. "Thank you, sir! He'll really appreciate a present from you!"

"That will be all for now," Don Pucci said.

Arthur returned to his customer.

Don Pucci glanced at Mario. "Make a note. Send a gift to the kid. He'll be ten, so make it a toy fire engine. The biggest you can buy."

"Consider it done," Mario said.

Don Pucci stared at Blade. "Now to business. Out of courtesy I came down to meet you. I don't want any trouble in my casino. And I understand you believe you have a grievance against me."

"We came to see you because we believed you were responsible for abducting Helen's daughter," Blade explained. "But the man who kidnapped Mindy did not look anything like you."

Don Pucci folded his hands under his chin. "Why did you suspect me?"

"Because the man gave your name," Blade disclosed.

The Don stiffened. "He used my name?"

Blade absently stared at the crowd, striving to unravel the mystery of Mindy's abduction, to piece together the parts of the puzzle. Why would someone take Mindy and claim to be Don Pucci? He noticed four men in suits and hats casually moving through the crowd in the direction of the bar. Each man was approximately 15 to 20 yards apart, as if they were trying to convey the impression of being alone. He sensed they were working in tandem, and his Warrior's instinct sounded a siren warning in his mind.

Don Pucci's men had not noticed. Most of them were concentrating on the Warriors.

Blade was cradling the Commando in his arms. He carefully slid his trigger finger through the trigger guard.

"I want to know everything about this man," Don Pucci was saying. "But not here. I would like you to come up to my quarters."

The four men were within ten yards of the Don's party. Each man had a hand under his suit coat.

Blade knew he had mere seconds to react. If he cut loose, the Don's men would gun him down. If he did nothing, the Don would be assassinated and the Warriors would lose a potential ally in their search for Mindy. Before he could rationalize a course of action, the four men confirmed their hostile intent.

Three of them pulled pistols, the fourth a sawed-off shotgun, and in unison they charged!

CHAPTER TWELVE

Don Giorgio's suite on the third floor of his Palace was furnished much like the casino; it was tawdry and pretentious. The carpet was off-green, the walls orange and blue. All of the furniture was polished to a sheen.

Hickok cautiously followed Kenney into the Don's inner sanctum, the Pythons cocked, anticipating a trap. They crossed a large room containing only 14 empty chairs, evidently a waiting room for those with appointments to see the Don, or the room where the button men congregated to await the Don's orders. The second room they encountered, a spacious office, was likewise unoccupied.

"This is my office," Kenney commented.

They came to a closed wooden door and halted.

Kenney rapped three times. "It's me," he announced. "He has me covered."

"Come in," a gruff voice declared.

Kenney opened the door and a Python barrel touched the back of his neck.

"Go real slow," Hickok advised.

Kenney shuffled into the next room, a huge chamber

with thick carpeting, several maple chairs, a sofa, and a wide desk aligned against the opposite wall.

Hickok kept his left Colt against Kenney's neck as he vigilantly advanced into Don Giorgio's office.

Three men were already there.

Seated behind the maple desk was a man with a strikingly harsh visage. He had steely, hawkish brown eyes and exceptionally bushy brows. His mouth was a thin slit, his hair black and slicked. He wore a black suit. An aura of palpable menace enshrouded him.

This, Hickok instinctively knew, was Don Giorgio.

A youngish man in a brown suit stood to the right of the desk, his arms folded across his chest. He had green eyes and a pointed chin.

A trigger man, Hickok guessed.

The man standing to the left of the desk was older, with streaks of gray in his otherwise brown hair. His cheeks and chin sagged, as if his skin was too tired to support his face. His brown eyes nervously examined the Warrior. He was wearing a dark blue suit.

Another hit man, Hickok reasoned.

The man behind the desk extended his arms in a friendly fashion, palms outward. "There's no need for the hardware, friend! I invited you up here to talk."

Hickok gave Kenney a shove.

Kenney stumbled several feet, then caught himself and turned. "There was no need for that," he said.

Hickok motioned with his Colts to the left.

Kenney took five steps to the left.

Hickok stared at the man behind the desk. "So you want to shoot the breeze?"

"I'm Don Giorgio," the man stated haughtily.

"I know who you are," Hickok said. "But I don't know why I should let you live."

"Let me live?" Giorgio repeated in surprise. "I asked you to come here as a token of my good will, and now you want to waste me?"

Hickok pointed both Pythons at the Don.

Giorgio, to his credit, didn't so much as flinch. But the

other three tensed, the young one dropping his hands to his sides and glaring at the gunslinger.

"I heard you aim to plug my pards and me for shootin' your two-bit, four-flushin' son," Hickok stated.

Giorgio's face reddened and his eyes narrowed. He seemed to wrestle with his emotions for a moment, then was calm. "Franky always was a hothead. He was always getting into fights over trifles. I tried to teach him not to sweat the small stuff, but he wouldn't listen." Giorgio paused. "The Enforcers report his death was a fair and square. Technically, I have no right to hold his death against you."

"Get to the point," Hickok prompted.

"The point, Mister . . ." Giorgio began, then stopped. "What is your name, anyway?"

"He says his name is Earp," Kenney answered. "Wyatt Earp."

Giorgio's forehead creased as he stared at the gunman. "Mr. Earp, then. I wanted you to know I'm forgoing my right to petition the Council for a sanction to snuff you."

"This must be my lucky day," Hickok quipped. "Why?"

"Why look a gift horse in the mouth?" Giorgio rejoined. "You should be grateful I'm not claiming my blood right."

"Why?" Hickok repeated his question.

Giorgio leaned back in his chair. "It would be bad business to whack you. By tonight everyone in Las Vegas will have heard about Franky, and they'll know his death was a fair and square. If I take action against you, I hurt my own reputation. Oh, I could call for a Council of the Dons and ask for a sanction to hit you. Every Don can ask for a Council whenever a grievance arises. I could present my case and demand a vote, and if the other Dons agreed and Don Pucci okayed the decision, you would be dead by morning. But word would get around. People would whisper behind my back. They would say I'd done wrong because Franky's death was a fair and square. Do you follow me?"

"So you won't kill me because it would be bad for your reputation and your business?" Hickok queried critically.

"That's it in a nutshell," Don Giorgio said.

Hickok snickered. "So much for family devotion."

"What do you say?" Giorgio asked. "Do we shake hands and call it quits?"

"Not so fast," Hickok said. "What about the runt downstairs?"

"I didn't tell him to try and gun you down," Giorgio replied. "He did that on his own. I don't like gunplay in my casino. It affects the trade."

"Then I'm free to go?" Hickok inquired.

Giorgio nodded. "And I want you to know there's no hard feelings. In fact, I'd like you to spend time in my casino as my personal guest. All the chips and eats will be on me. What do you say?"

Hickok twirled the Colts into their holsters. "How can I refuse an offer like that?"

"Kenney will take you downstairs," Giorgio said. "He'll provide you with everything you need."

"Thanks," Hickok stated. He backed toward the door.

"Can you wait for me in the hallway?" Kenney asked the gunman. "I'll be there in a minute."

"No problem," Hickok responded. He hooked his thumbs in his gunbelt and strolled out.

Kenney moved to the door and watched until the gunfighter had passed through his office, the waiting room, and closed the hall door behind him. He faced the Don. "Before I take that clown downstairs, I need to know what's going on."

"Yeah, boss," Sacks chimed in. "I don't get none of this. How come you're letting that scumbag live after he snuffed Franky?"

Giorgio gazed at Kenney. "I want you to treat him to a good time. You know who he is, don't you?"

Kenney nodded. "I figured it out. He's one of those Warriors. Hickok, right?"

"Right," Giorgio verified. "Which means the Warriors are already in Vegas. Give him anything he wants. Find

Nadine. Tell her to hit on him. I want him to spend the night. If he leaves the Palace, I'm to be informed immediately. Understand?"

"Got you," Kenney answered. He wheeled and departed.

Sacks shook his head, clearly bemused. "I don't get none of this, boss."

"I hate to admit it," Ozzi chimed in, "but neither do I."

"Then I'll have to explain it to you," Giorgio said. "I don't want my lieutenants in the dark, so I'll spell everything out." He paused and stared at Ozzi. "Do you remember about a year ago, when that drifter lost a couple of grand at poker and couldn't pay up?"

"Sure I do," Ozzi said. "You were going to have me break his legs."

"That was the one," Giorgio confirmed. "He tried to trade information in exchange for cancelling his debt. He claimed he knew about a Federation which might pose a threat to the Dons. He said this Freedom Federation, as it's called, planned to consolidate their forces and conquer the western half of what was once the United States. He told me all about this Federation, about the different factions in it. I found his information very, very interesting, and I later verified most of it. There is a Freedom Federation, and they do have a protective association, of sorts. But they're no threat to the Dons."

"Do the other Dons know about this Federation?" Ozzi queried.

"I don't know," Giorgio replied. "I don't think so. This Federation has kept pretty much to itself, all except for one faction. They're known as the Family."

Sacks grinned and slapped his right thigh. "They're the ones in Minnesota! The ones who live at the Home!"

"Give the man a cigar!" Giorgio cracked. "Yeah. The very same. I discovered they have a heavy rep, especially their fighters, the Warriors. These Warriors have taken on the Ruskies, the Technics, even the Doktor, and they came out on top every time. The more I learned about these Warriors, the more convinced I became that they were the ones to help me snuff Pucci."

"Now you lost me," Sacks said.

"I'm not surprised," Giorgio stated dryly. "Anyway, I sent out feelers to all my sources. I learned all I could about the Warriors. I even found out some of their names: Blade, Hickok, Geronimo, Yama, Rikki, and Bertha. And I discovered a pattern."

"What kind of pattern?" Ozzi questioned.

Giorgio smiled. "Simply this. Every time the Home was attacked, or any time Family members were whacked, or kidnapped, or even just injured, the Warriors went after the party responsible. No matter what the odds, no matter how badly they were outnumbered or outgunned, the Warriors *always* made the offenders pay. They always exacted retribution," he said with sincere admiration.

"They sound like us," Sacks commented.

Giorgio snorted. "They are nothing like us. Their Family and our Families are as different as night and day. They believe in a lot of spiritual garbage, and they don't know the value of power and money. But the Warriors are as deadly a bunch of professionals as you'd ever want to meet. They're tops."

"You sound like you respect them," Ozzie remarked.

"I do," Giorgio responded. "Don't ever underestimate them."

"Even the bozo in the buckskins?" Ozzi asked.

"Especially him," Giorgio answered. "He may come across as a dummy, but I hear it's all an act. Hickok is one of the deadliest Warriors."

"He's a fast son of a bitch," Sacks mentioned. "Did you see him on the monitor when he shot Dirkson?"

"I saw him," Ozzi said.

"If you two are finished flapping your gums," Giorgio declared, "I'd like to continue."

"Sorry, boss," Sacks said.

"You didn't tell us all this before you took us to Minnesota," Ozzi noted. "You didn't tell us a thing until we were on the road, and then all you said was that we were going to make an important snatch, and that our

Family would be taking over Vegas. You kept saying the snatch was important, but you never told us the reason. How come you're coming clean now?"

"Necessity," Giorgio responded. "I didn't tell anyone about my plans to go to Minnesota except for Kenney because I didn't want a leak. I didn't want Pucci to find out what I was up to. And I had to tell Kenney because I left him in charge of my operations while I was gone." He paused. "Now, everything has changed. My plan isn't working the way I thought it would. We could be in for some rough weather, and I want my top men aware of the situation."

"Gee, boss," Sacks interjected. "Thanks for the compliment."

Giorgio sighed. "Anyway, I devised a scheme to use the Warriors to whack Pucci. I figured I could snatch one of the Family, pin the blame on Pucci, and the Warriors would take care of the rest. Considering their heavy rep, I knew they'd come after whoever we kidnapped. I expected them to come to Vegas, look up Pucci, and that would be that." He grinned at the deviousness of his plot.

"That would be what, boss?" Sacks wanted to know.

"The Warriors would take care of Pucci for me," Giorgio replied impatiently. "I've tried three times in the past eight years to whack that bastard, and each time I failed. The last attempt put him in a wheelchair for life, but I want him dead! I should be the top Don in Vegas, not that old prick! He doesn't deserve to rule Vegas! He's old, he's past his prime, and he should be put out to pasture. And I'm the man who's going to do it!"

"What about the Warriors?" Ozzi queried. "You said your plan isn't working."

"Hickok is here, so some of the other Warriors must be here too. But I haven't heard anything about them making a hit on Pucci. Instead, I hear about these four strangers responsible for killing Franky. I got descriptions of the four, but I didn't put two and two together until Hickok came into the Palace," Giorgio said. "When I saw him on the monitor, I remembered the description I was given on the Warriors. Blade is supposed to be a big guy who always packs Bowies. Hickok wear buckskins and pearl-handled Colts. And one of the guys who whacked Franky's crew was a giant with knives. Then a man in buckskins shows up in my joint and uses a phony name. That clinched it!"

"He used a phony name?" Sacks interrupted.

"Wyatt Earp, remember?" Giorgio reminded him.

"Oh. Yeah. How'd you know it was phony?" Sacks inquired.

Giorgio shook his head in disgust. "Because I went to school, dummy. Wyatt Earp was one of the guys we studied in history class. He was sort of an ancient wiseguy."

"Do you think the Warriors know you set them up to kill Pucci?" Ozzi asked. "Do you think they hit Franky on purpose?"

"No," Giorgio said. "The Enforcers and the witnesses swear Franky started it. Franky goaded them into the fight. The jackass! He was an insult to my lineage!"

"But he was your only son!" Sacks stated.

"Don't remind me!" Giorgio snapped. "I should have spent more time with him when he was a kid. He was a spoiled brat, and he didn't know what it meant to be a made man. If he'd played his cards right, he could have inherited my empire. Once I take out Pucci, I'll go after the other Dons. Everyone says the Seven Families War eighty years ago was bloody and horrible, but they haven't seen a thing yet! By the time I'm through, the Seven Families War will seem like a picnic!"

"Why haven't the Warriors snuffed Pucci yet?" Ozzi asked.

"I don't know," Giorgio admitted. "But I'm not sitting on my ass waiting for them to hit the prick! I've hired a hit squad of independents to take care of Pucci if he shows his face in the casino."

"What about Hickok? Why is he here?" Ozzi probed.

Giorgio pondered for a moment. "He came to see if I wanted revenge for Franky."

"And do you?" Ozzi questioned.

Giorgio's mouth twisted downward. "Of course! Franky was a moron, but he was blood. I'll keep tabs on Hickok, try to find out where the rest of the Warriors are, and if they've outlived their usefulness to me, I'll have them whacked."

"Gee, boss," Sacks said. "You think of everything. If the Warriors whack Don Pucci, no one will think to blame you. You can take over Vegas without the other Dons ganging up on you."

"I'll do it one way or the other," Giorgio vowed. "Pucci's Family isn't as strong as it was eighty years ago. If the Warriors waste him, the other Dons will easily come under my thumb. But even if the Warriors blow it, Pucci *is* going down. I will be the top Don by the end of the year."

Ozzi straightened attentively. "With your indulgence, there's a matter I'd like to discuss with you."

Giorgio smirked. "As if I couldn't guess."

"I respectfully ask your permission," Ozzi said.

"I knew this was coming," Giorgio commented. "I saw the way you were looking at her all the way back from Minnesota. And I saw you threaten to rack Nicky if he laid his hands on her."

"Will you consent?" Ozzi asked.

"Why do you want her? She's an outsider," Giorgio remarked. "Why not pick one of the local girls? You could have the cream of the crop. You're a made man. A big wheel in my organization."

"I want Mindy," Ozzi stated.

"What do you see in her?" Giorgio inquired.

"I don't know how to describe my feelings," Ozzi responded. "I've never felt like this before."

Giorgio grinned. "Some call it love. I call it lust. If you want to marry her, she's yours. But there are two conditions."

"Name them," Ozzi said eagerly.

"First, you wait until this Warrior business is resolved," Giorgio directed.

"As you wish," Ozzi stated dutifully.

"Second, you convince her the marriage is in her best

interests," Giorgio said. "She's a little hellcat when she gets her temper up. I don't want one of my lieutenants dragging his betrothed down the aisle the day of the wedding. Everyone would talk."

"I'll convince her she loves me," Ozzi pledged. "Even if I must slap her around a bit. She'll get the message."

"You have the right attitude," Giorgio said approvingly. "A woman needs to be slapped around now and then to keep her in line. Sock her in the gut. That usually works for me. They don't like to be bruised, so you've got to be careful when you hit her in the face."

"Can I go see her now?" Ozzi queried.

"Go ahead."

"What about me, boss?" Sacks asked.

"I want you to go down to the casino," Giorgio directed. "Keep an eye on Hickok. Send Kenney up to me."

"Okay," Sacks said.

"I'll give the Warriors until tomorrow to off Don Pucci," Giorgio remarked. "If they don't, I can only assume they don't intend to kill him. I'll put out a contract on every Warrior in town."

Ozzi and Sacks exited the room.

Don Giorgio stared at the doorway, reflecting. Ozzi was one of his best button men, but the kid was soft in the noodle. Imagine being dumb enough to fall for the skirt from the family! Mindy was a liability, incriminating evidence. The girl had to be snuffed, and Kenney was just the man to do it. An accident could be arranged. The poor bimbo would hang herself from a light fixture. All Kenney would need to do would be arrange a scheduling snafu so the girl's room was unguarded for a while.

Ozzi would be heartbroken.

But those were the breaks!

CHAPTER THIRTEEN

The four hit men were closing in on Don Pucci's party.
Blade did the only thing he could do; he suddenly crouched in front of the Don's wheelchair, aimed the Commando barrel over Pucci's right shoulder, and sighted on one of the trigger men with a pistol, the nearest one.

Startled, the Don's eight men swung their machine guns at the giant. Afraid of hitting the Don, they held their fire.

Blade cut loose, the Commando chattering loudly, the stock bucking against his shoulder.

The closest hit man took a burst in the chest and was flung to the carpet.

Mario swung in the direction Blade had fired.

Don Pucci's hands were sliding under the red blanket in his lap. Several of his men started toward him.

The hit man with the sawed-off shotgun let fly into the back of one of the Don's men at point-blank range, the buckshot blowing the man's chest out and sending him sprawling. Pivoting, the hit man took a bead on the Don.

Blade squeezed the trigger, stitching the shotgun-wielding killer from the crotch to the forehead.

One of the two remaining hit men shot a pair of the Don's guards and aimed at the Don.

The last hit man was barreling toward the wheelchair.

Caught unawares by the abrupt assassination attempt, with their attention focused on the Warriors, none of the Don's men had fired a shot in the first three seconds of the attack. Now, as they realized the true danger was coming at them from the crowds, not the bar, they spun to confront the last two hit men. But they were too slow.

Geronimo and Helen fired simultaneously. Geronimo's Browning struck the hit man on the right in the face and he crashed onto his back. Helen's Armalite sent a half-dozen rounds into the last hit man, into the left side of his chest. He twisted and toppled over.

In the aftermath of the shooting, the casino was as quiet as a tomb.

Blade slowly stood.

Don Pucci turned his wheelchair and scrutinized the four dead hit men, then glanced at his own casualties. He gazed up at the giant. "Thanks. They nearly nailed me."

"Do you know who they were?" Blade asked.

"No," Don Pucci said. "But I'll find out. They were probably sent by Giorgio, but I'll never be able to prove it. He'd hire outside talent for a job like this. He'd never use any of his own men."

"Why does Giorgio want to kill you?" Blade queried.

"Why else?" Pucci responded. "He wants to take over Vegas. But I can't do anything about him unless I can uncover some proof. I must justify my actions to the other Dons."

"I thought you are running the show in Vegas," Blade observed. "Why must you justify your actions to them?"

"Courtesy," Don Pucci said. "If I don't show them respect, they're not about to show me any respect. All the Dons belong to the Council, our governing body. If any of us has a grievance against another Don, we bring it up in Council. If I was to hit Giorgio without a justifiable grievance and the agreement of the Council, an all-out war could result." He glanced at Mario, then nodded toward the bodies. "Clean up this mess. Discover who they were. And send ten grand to the families of each of our boys who were whacked."

Mario hurried off, barking orders to the Don's men.

The casino came alive again, gradually, the customers mingling and conversing as the gambling resumed.

"You took this calmly," Blade said, praising the Don.

Don Pucci sighed. "This has happened before. Why do you think I'm in this damn wheelchair?"

Blade stared at the body of the hit man with the shotgun. "What if they had gotten past your men?"

Don Pucci's hands came out from under the red blanket. Clutched in his right was an Eagle 357 Magnum pistol. "I'm confined to a wheelchair, but I'm not helpless."

Helen stepped up to the wheelchair. "Do you know where my daughter is?"

"I wish I did," Don Pucci replied. "I owe you for saving my life. I'll do anything I can to help." He reached up and gingerly touched his right ear, smiling at Blade. "That piece of yours almost ruptured my eardrum. I can hardly hear for all the ringing."

"Sorry," Blade said.

"Don't apologize," Pucci remarked. "I'm alive, aren't I?" He paused. "Now, about this kidnapping business. I'm not involved, but if you give me time, I will try and find out who is behind it."

Blade watched the Don's men removing the corpses. Two men in jeans and T-shirt were approaching, bearing buckets and mops to soak up the puddles of blood. He saw eight or nine people playing a row of slot machines, and he wondered how they could callously disregard the bloodshed they'd just seen. How could they become so engrossed in the slot machines so soon after witnessing the shootout? Why were the slot machines so fascinating? He recalled the token Mario had given him, the one in his left front pocket. If the opportunity arose, he intended to use the token and learn the secret of the slot machines firsthand. He . . .

The token!

Blade abruptly remembered the *other* token in his possession, the one in his back pocket, the one he had found on the corpse in Halma, the one from the man killed at the kidnapping scene. He reached into the pocket and fished out the blue token, then held it up to read the words printed on both sides: JOHNNY'S PALACE.

What a fool he'd been!

Blade suddenly perceived the reason for his previous ambiguous feelings of unease. The answer had been staring him in the face the whole time, figuratively speaking, and he'd been too dense to notice! Why would the man found dead near Halma have a token from Don Giorgio's casino *unless he frequented that casino!* He looked down at Don Pucci. "Would one of your men gamble in Giorgio's casino?"

Don Pucci snorted. "None of my men would be caught dead in Giorgio's joint. The games there are rigged."

"What about Giorgio's men?" Blade probed. "Would they gamble in *your* casino?"

Don Pucci shook his head. "Not likely. I don't trust any of Pucci's men. They rarely come in here, because if they do I have one of my boys stick with them like glue. It makes them too uncomfortable." He squinted at Blade for a moment. "Why are you asking all these questions?"

"There were three people with Helen's daughter when she was abducted," Blade detailed. "Two of them were murdered. We also found the body of a stranger. And on his body I found this." He flipped the token to the Don.

Don Pucci deftly caught it and inspected the token. His lips compressed and his nostrils flared.

"One more thing," Blade said, acting on his hunch. "What does Don Giorgio look like?"

"How should I describe him?" Don Pucci replied. "He has black hair and brown eyes. He's a heartless bastard, the meanest-looking son of a bitch you'd ever want to meet."

Ted's word came back to Blade in a rush. "His hair was black, his eyes brown. His face was kind of mean looking." He placed his right hand on his forehead and stared at the floor.

Geronimo nudged his friend's right elbow. "What's the matter?"

"Blade? What is it?" Helen added.

Blade removed his hand, his countenance set in a chiseled mask of suppressed indignation. "We were set up," he said huskily.

"What are you talking about?" Helen asked, perplexed.

"Don Pucci didn't take Mindy," Blade elaborated. "Don Giorgio did. Giorgio is using us. He probably hoped we'd barge into this casino and confront Don Pucci. Why else was Ted told we could find Mindy at the Golden Crown Casino?"

"Then Mindy isn't here?" Helen queried, distraught by the revelation.

Blade shook his head.

"Giorgio wanted us to kill Pucci for him," Geronimo deduced.

"That's my guess," Blade concurred.

"If Mindy isn't here, where is she?" Helen inquired.

"I can answer that," Don Pucci interjected. "If Giorgio took your daughter to set you up to whack me, then she's either in his joint or dead."

"Oh, no!" Helen said mournfully.

"If you take him on, if you try to locate the girl in his casino, he'll kill her for sure," Don Pucci stated. "He's not about to leave around any evidence connecting him to this caper."

Helen looked at Blade. "What do we do?"

"We need to come up with a plan," Blade replied.

"He's right," Don Pucci said. "You must play it cagey. If you rush over to the Palace, Mindy is as good as dead. If Giorgio spots any of you in his joint, he'll snuff her."

The three Warriors exchanged startled glances.

"Hickok!" Blade exclaimed.

"Who is this Hickok?" Don Pucci questioned.

"He's a Warrior, like us," Blade answered. "And he's in Giorgio's casino right this moment!"

"Then God help Mindy," the Don stated grimly.

CHAPTER FOURTEEN

"How many cards do you want, hick?" the professional gambler asked. He was holding the deck in his left hand.

Hickok glanced at the ring of spectators watching the game. Over an hour ago they had started gathering, after word of his winning streak had circulated around the casino. Initially, six players had been in the game, but one by one Hickok had eliminated them. Now only the arrogant gambler remained, and it was his turn to deal.

"Come on, hick," the gambler said, baiting the gunfighter. "I don't have all day."

Hickok deliberately stalled. How much longer, he wondered, did he need to stay in Giorgio's casino? How much time did he need to buy Blade and the others? It would be dark soon. Surely they had found Mindy by now. But if so, why hadn't one of them shown up to let him know? He glanced at the Henry, leaning against the table to his left.

"How many cards?" the gambler repeated.

Hickok gazed at his hand. Three kings, a four, and a nine. He discarded the four and the nine. "Two."

The gambler dealt two cards to the gunman.

Hickok picked up the cards and almost laughed aloud. The two of spades and the two of diamonds! He had a full house!

"Dealer takes three," the gambler said, and did so.

Hickok was beginning to worry about his friends. He had stayed in the Palace to insure he was the focus of Giorgio's attention. Sure enough, he'd been under surveillance all day. He suspected they would shadow him if he departed the casino, and he didn't want to lead Giorgio's men to his fellow Warriors. But he was growing weary of waiting, and he was extremely concerned for Blade, Geronimo, and Helen. What if they were in trouble? He decided to give them until nightfall, then go looking for them, shadows or no shadows.

"Are you playing or daydreaming?" the gambler snapped.

Hickok smiled sweetly. This varmint was going to get his, real soon! "It'll cost you to stay in the game, Big-Mouth. Five hundred." He counted out the chips and added them to the pot.

The gambler studied the man in buckskins. He was convinced the blond man was a country bumpkin, and he was determined to show the upstart how the game of poker was played by a real pro. "You're not bluffing me, mister. I'll match your five hundred."

Hickok watched the gambler slide five hundred to the center of the table.

"What do you have?" the gambler asked belligerently.

Hickok laid his cards on the table, face up. "Read 'em and weep, sucker."

The gambler looked like he was choking. He turned crimson and sputtered, then dropped his hand on the table in disgust.

Hickok reached out and claimed the pot. "Stick around. I'll give you some lessons on how to play this game." He grinned at the recollection of the many hours he'd spent playing card games at the Home. Rummy. Gin. Pinochle. Poop on Your Neighbor. Fish. Poker. Many others. The

Family members never actually gambled; they played for the sheer fun of playing. And as an avid student of the Old West, Hickok's favorite game was poker.

"Damn you!" the gambler suddenly barked. He stood, shoving his chair backwards.

The spectators scurried away from the table.

"You shouldn't gamble if you're a poor loser," Hickok remarked.

"You son of a bitch!" the gambler spat out. He swept the right flap of his coat aside, revealing a Charter Arms Bulldog revolver in a holster on his right hip. "On your feet!"

Hickok slowly rose, his hands resting on the table. "If you apologize, real nice like, you'll live to play cards again some day."

The gambler snorted contemptuously. "Apologize! You can kiss my ass first!"

"I wouldn't touch your butt with a brandin' iron," Hickok retorted.

A new voice intruded on their dispute. "Hold it right there!" Giorgio's right-hand man, Kenney, hurried up to the table. "Murphy, you've been warned about your temper before!" he admonished the gambler. "And you know the rules. No gunplay."

"Hang the rules!" Murphy declared. "This is between him and me!"

"The Don will not appreciate this," Kenney noted.

"I'm not backing down to this hick!" Murphy said angrily.

Hickok's blue eyes became flinty. "Are you going to pull your iron, or are you aimin' to insult me to death?"

Murphy went for his revolver, his right hand sweeping down and up in a practiced draw, a draw he'd employed on 14 occasions to kill a foe. He was leveling the barrel when he was shocked to see twin Colts materialize in the hick's hands.

Hickok fired both Pythons, the Magnums thundering. The heavy slugs bored into the gambler's face, making cavities of his cheeks, and blew out the rear of his cranium.

Murphy was hurled to the floor, his body landing spread-eagled. Chunks of flesh and bits of hair dotted the carpet around him.

Kenney gazed at the dead gambler. "Murphy had quite a rep," he commented, then looked at the Warrior. "And you beat him."

Hickok twirled the Pythons into their holsters. "Piece of cake."

"You have a knack for racking up a body count," Kenney remarked.

"If some coyote is plannin' to perforate me," Hickok noted, "I don't intend to oblige them."

"We'll clean up the mess," Kenney offered. "How are you fixed? Do you want more chips?"

"No," Hickok said, glancing at the stakes he had won. "I already have a heap." He picked up the Henry and slung it over his back.

"Looks to me like you have over five thousand there," Kenney said as he scrutinized the piles on the table. "Do you want me to cash them for you?"

Hickok shrugged. "Why not. I'll mosey around the casino." He ambled off, heading for the slot machines. What should he play next? He'd spent the afternoon at various card games, capped off by his three-hour poker match. Boredom was setting in. He couldn't understand how folks could spend so much time gambling. Playing cards at the Home for the sheer fun of it was one thing, but gambling was entirely different. When a person played for money, when valuables were at stake, the game lost its entertaining, recreational quality. Instead, a simple, relaxing pastime became a serious business of winning at all costs. The gambler had epitomized such an attitude; to Murphy, winning was everything, even at the cost of his life.

A middle-aged couple was playing one of the slots.

Hickok stopped and watched them. He casually scanned the casino, searching for his tail.

Fifteen yards away a young mobster in a beige suit was gazing overhead at a chandelier as if the fixture was the most interesting item in the universe.

Hickok grinned and walked over to the hit man. "Howdy."

The young mobster was clearly ruffled by this unexpected development. He looked at the Warrior, blinking rapidly, then up at the chandelier.

"Cat got your tongue?" Hickok asked. "I said howdy."

"Hi," the man replied. He had black hair and dark eyes.

"Would you do me a favor?" Hickok inquired. "Would you find Kenney and get some tokens for me? I'd like to play the slot machines for a spell."

The mobster stared at the gunman. "I'm not your servant."

"No, but you have been shadowin' me," Hickok said.

"I don't know what you're talking about," the man responded.

"And I was born yesterday," Hickok cracked. "Look, we both know you've been tailin' me, and you must be gettin' as bored as I am if you're admirin' the lights. Don Giorgio told me I could have anything I wanted, and I want some tokens. I promise I'll stay right here until you return."

Although no one was within ten feet of them, the mobster lowered his voice. "But you're not supposed to know I'm following you!"

"Darn! Now you tell me!" Hickok said.

"If Kenney finds out you made me, I'm in hot water," the mobster divulged.

"I won't tell if you don't," Hickok pledged. "Now what about the tokens?"

"I'm not to let you out of my sight," the mobster said.

"I'm thinkin' of payin' Don Pucci's place a visit later," Hickok commented innocently. "You certainly can't follow me over there."

"Mister, my orders are to stick with you like glue," the mobster disclosed. "Where you go, I go."

"What if I have to tinkle?" Hickok queried.

"Then I'll tinkle too," the mobster replied.

Hickok started to turn, pleased at the confirmation of

his suspicion concerning the men assigned to shadow him. They *would* tail him if he left the Palace, which meant he had to lose them before leaving. And there was one more thing he needed to know. He gazed at the mobster. "I hope I didn't do anything to get you in trouble with your head honchos," he said with sincerity. "I know they're watchin' us on hidden cameras."

The mobster glanced around nervously. "Don Giorgio and Kenney don't spend all their time watching the monitor. Internal surveillance is conducted by Security from the Security Office. There's a hookup in the Don's office which he can tap into whenever he wants. But Kenney is working the floor, and the Don might not be watching."

"Then I'd best be gettin' along," Hickok said. He walked off, observing the patrons, calculating. He doubted the cameras would be trained on him the whole time. The tails were expected to keep an eye on him. If he could shake the shadows, and if he could leave the casino and head upstairs without the cameras observing him, he stood a good chance of locating another exit from the building. The front entrance was too risky. The Don was bound to have it covered.

But how could he get upstairs without causing a ruckus?

The answer came from an unexpected source.

Hickok was walking past the blackjack tables when he saw her again. The one with the nice teeth. The one who had walked by him five times during the afternoon. Each time she had smiled seductively and given him a come-hither look, and each time he had returned her smile and gone about his business. The last such incident had been prior to the poker game. She had sashayed up to him and requested a match to light her cigarette. He'd checked his pockets, told her he didn't have any matches, and walked off, leaving her with her rosy red lips gaping.

Now there she was again, watching a blackjack game.

She was about six feet tall, and she had been blessed with a body of abundant proportions in all the right places. Her hair was a dusty gold, worn down to the small of her back.

Her eyes were blue. The front of her red dress formed a V with the point touching her navel. When she leaned forward, her breasts threatened to make a bid for freedom. Her face was oval, her lashes long and lovely.

Hickok repressed a smirk and stepped up to her. "Howdy. Remember me?"

She turned, her eyes widening slightly before she recovered her composure. "I remember you," she said huskily. "You're the man who doesn't carry matches."

"The name is Earp," Hickok fibbed once more. "Wyatt Earp."

"Mr. Earp," she said softly. "I'm Nadine."

"That's a right pretty name, ma'am," he complimented her.

"Thank you, Mr. Earp," she said.

"Call me Hi . . ." Hickok began, then caught himself. "Wyatt."

Nadine grinned. "As you wish. What can I do for you?"

"I saw you standin' here and figured we could chew the fat," Hickok replied. "I don't have any friends here and I'm a mite lonely."

Nadine's grin became a wide smile, her white teeth glistening. "How sad."

"Do you mind if we shoot the breeze?" Hickok inquired politely. "I couldn't help but notice how friendly you were earlier."

"I didn't think you'd noticed me," Nadine said.

Hickok ran his eyes up and down her body. "How could anyone not notice a beautiful woman like you?"

Nadine was clearly pleased by his attention. She cleared her throat and gazed around the room.

Out of the corner of his left eye, Hickok saw Kenney 20 feet away, regarding them intently.

Nadine's head nodded once, almost imperceptibly.

Kenney beamed.

Hickok pretended to be immersed in the blackjack game for a few moments.

"Are you hungry?" Nadine asked.

"Nope," Hickok replied.

"Me neither," Nadine said. "And if we want to talk, we won't have much privacy in the casino."

"I don't know where else we could go," Hickok remarked artlessly.

"I do," Nadine stated. "I'm on vacation. I have a suite upstairs. If you don't mind, we could go up there and talk. I have some munchies in the fridge if you do get hungry."

"I don't know...." Hickok hedged. "What would your husband or boyfriend say?"

"I'm not married," Nadine answered. "And I don't have a boyfriend."

"Then I guess we can go up to your room," Hickok said, putting a nervous tinge in his voice.

Nadine looped her right arm in his left. "Don't be shy! I won't bite. We'll have fun together."

Hickok smiled at her. "I hope so."

Nadine led the gunman toward the elevators along the far wall. "Tell me about yourself," she coaxed him.

"There's not much to tell," Hickok said.

"Where are you from?"

"Oh, here and there," Hickok responded.

"What do you do for a living?" Nadine probed.

"This and that," Hickok answered.

Nadine's eyes narrowed. "I saw you tangle with Murphy," she mentioned.

"I hope it didn't shock your sensibilities," Hickok remarked decorously.

"No," Nadine said. "I've seen shootings before, but I've never seen anyone draw a gun as fast as you do." She paused. "Do you do everything so fast?"

Hickok chuckled. "Not everything."

"That's nice to hear," Nadine commented. "Some things should be done nice and slow."

"Like eatin' venison steak," Hickok said, and licked his lips.

Nadine laughed. "I was thinking of something else."

Hickok looked at her. "Oh? What?"

"I'll save it for a surprise," Nadine stated, and giggled.

"Oh, goody!" Hickok stated. "I love surprises!"

They reached the row of six elevators. Nadine pressed an UP button on the wall, and they took the first elevator which opened, the second from the right.

Nadine punched the button for the eighth floor. "I'm in 819," she mentioned.

The elevator door closed and they ascended.

Nadine squeezed Hickok's left arm playfully. "This is going to be fun!"

Hickok smiled. "You don't know the half of it."

CHAPTER FIFTEEN

Blade, Geronimo, and Helen stood quietly next to the huge windows overlooking the glittering city. Dusk enshrouded the landscape, and the nearly infinite variety of Vegas's neon lights had flared to life. To the three Warriors from the Home, where kerosene lanterns were a luxury at night, the impression was dazzling.

Blade turned and faced the doorway to the moderately sized chamber as the door opened and the Dons filed inside. The five men were a curious mixture of statures and physiques.

A large, circular wooden table filled the center of the room. Six wooden chairs ringed the table at regular intervals. Seated in his wheelchair near the windows, his hands on the table, his back to the Warriors, was Don Pucci. The token from Johnny's Palace was clenched in his left hand.

The five Dons halted when they saw the Warriors.

"What the hell is this?" demanded a portly, bald man in a white suit. "Council meetings are to be conducted in private. No soldiers. No Consiglioris. No one else."

"With your indulgence, Don Marchese," Don Pucci said. "I have called this emergency meeting of the Council, and these people are present at my invitation. Their testimony is essential to the topic we will discuss."

Another Don, a small man with brown hair and eyes, attired in an immaculate blue suit and shining, black patent leather shoes, spoke up. "What is this topic, Don Pucci?"

"We are here, Don Lansky, to discuss the danger of Las Vegas being attacked by a Federation army," Don Pucci replied.

The Dons exchanged startled glances.

"Vegas is going to be attacked?" Don Marchese queried in astonishment.

"Please," Don Pucci said, gesturing at the chairs. "Have a seat. Everything will be explained."

The Dons quickly sat down.

Don Pucci angled his wheelchair so he could see the Warriors and the table. "First, I must make the introductions." He waved his right hand at the Warriors. "These three are Warriors from a compound called the Home located in Minnesota."

With raking stares, the Dons scrutinized the newcomers.

Don Pucci went on. "Their leader is Blade, the big one. The Indian is Geronimo. The broad is Helen."

"Why are they here?" asked a man in a green suit with a ragged scar on his left cheek.

"I'm getting to that, Don Siegel," Don Pucci stated. He motioned for Blade to step over to the table.

Blade complied, the Commando slung over his shoulders, his hands on the hilts of his Bowies. "Hello, gentlemen," he said.

Don Pucci pointed at the Dons, introducing them one by one, going from right to left. "This is Don Marchese, then Don Lansky." He indicated a stocky man in brown with a bulbous nose and a sloping forehead. "Don Cuascut. Don Siegel." Next he pointed at a lean man in a gray suit. "And, finally, Don Talone."

"Wait a minute," Don Talone said in a high-pitched

voice. "Where is Don Giorgio? We can not hold a Council meeting without all of the Dons present. You know the rules."

"Don Giorgio will arrive in a half hour," Don Pucci explained. "I wanted to have thirty minutes to ourselves. You'll understand why in a few moments."

"This isn't proper," Don Talone said.

Don Pucci smiled benignly. "Don Talone, your friendship with Don Giorgio is well known and we can appreciate your loyalty. However, in this instance your loyalty is misplaced. Thanks to your friend, we are in jeopardy of having the Freedom Federation declare war on us."

"What is the Freedom Federation?" Don Lansky asked.

Don Pucci nodded at Blade. "Would you do the honors?"

"The Freedom Federation is an alliance of seven factions," Blade detailed. "Three of the factions, the Family, the Clan, and the Moles, are all located in what was once Minnesota. Our allies include the Flathead Indians in Montana and the Cavalry in the Dakota Territory. Our two largest members are the Civilized Zone and the Free State of California."

"I've heard of the Federation," Don Siegel mentioned. "Why would they want to give us any grief?"

Don Pucci frowned. "Because one of us is responsible for kidnapping a young woman from the Family," he answered.

Blade studied the expressions on the Dons. They were each digesting the news with a calm, but somber, detachment. All except for Giorgio's friend, Talone. He was biting his lower lip nervously.

"The Warriors and I spent the afternoon together," Don Pucci went on. "I am convinced their grievance is genuine. If we don't show them respect and help them, they could take their case to the Federation leaders. Do we want to risk having a Federation army sent against us?"

"Hold the phone," Don Marchese said. "We have high-ranking visitors from California and the Civilized Zone all the time. We pay them good money to insure they don't meddle in our affairs—"

"But this time *we* have meddled in *theirs*," Don Pucci said, interrupting.

Blade was hoping Don Marchese would continue. He wanted to learn about the high-ranking visitors from the Family's allies.

"What exactly is their grievance?" Don Siegel inquired.

Don Pucci looked at Blade. "Tell them about the snatch."

Blade spent five minutes describing the abduction of Mindy. None of the Dons spoke until he was finished.

"This is deplorable!" Don Lansky stated. "We have a standing rule not to involve outsiders in our affairs."

"How do we know one of us is involved?" Don Talone questioned. "The evidence is not concrete. Someone could be setting us up."

"Someone was setup, all right," Don Pucci said. "This was found on the body of the stranger found at the kidnapping scene." He tossed the token to Don Marchese.

Each of the Dons took a turn at examining the token.

Don Talone, the last to inspect it, laughed. "A token? This is your evidence? This doesn't mean a thing. Anyone can obtain a token."

"There is one more thing," Don Pucci said coldly. "Something the Warriors didn't even think of. Something I discovered when I was looking at the address book."

"What address book?" Don Marchese queried.

"The address book they found on th body of the man with the token," Don Pucci elaborated. He extended his right hand toward Blade. "May I?"

Blade reached into his right rear pocket and withdrew the small black address book. He gave it to the Don.

Don Pucci waved the book. "This is the incriminating evidence linking one of us to the kidnapping."

"A lousy address book?" Don Talone remarked sarcastically.

Don Pucci's features became rigid. "This lousy address book has the name and address of its owner written on the inside of the front cover." He slid the address book to Don

Marchese. "Enlighten all of us."

Don Marchese picked up the book and opened it. He stared at the handwriting for several seconds, his lips twitching in budding anger.

"What does it say?" Don Siegel prompted.

"Property of . . ." Don Marchese said, reading the writing. "Alberto Manzo. 6415 Roseway Avenue."

"Manzo!" Don Lansky exclaimed. "He was one of Giorgio's button men."

"This still doesn't prove Don Giorgio was involved," Don Talone said.

"It does for me," Don Pucci stated.

"The evidence is incriminating," Don Cuascut commented, "but not conclusive."

"How much more do you need?" Don Pucci asked. He surveyed the men at the table. "Do you have any idea of the gravity of the situation? We risk antagonizing a strong alliance with a powerful military force. We risk the Federation marching on Vegas. Do you want that?"

Don Talone snickered. "You're exaggerating."

"Am I?" Don Pucci rejoined. "Let me remind you of a few facts. We have several thousand soldiers, all told. We're strong, but we don't have a standing army, per se. We've survived for so long because of two conditions. First, we never meddle in the affairs of outsiders. Never. For over a century we have honored this rule. Second, we've paid off the necessary people to guarantee we're left alone. But the officials in California and the Civilized Zone on our payroll will not look kindly on having a young woman from one of their allies kidnapped by one of us."

"If she was," Don Talone interjected.

"Don Giorgio's animosity toward me is no secret," Don Pucci said. "Everyone here knows he wants to oust me. He couldn't try a direct hit with his own button men, because he knows many of you are close friends of mine and he would face your combined wrath. Someone—and let's, for the sake of argument, assume Giorgio is responsible—has hired independents to whack me. Four times, no less!"

"Four?" Don Lansky said.

"There was another attempt earlier," Don Pucci disclosed. "The Warriors saved me."

"I heard about it," Don Marchese mentioned. "I am sorry."

"The outside talent hasn't been able to do the job," Don Pucci said. "So now someone—and, again, who else but Giorgio would do it?—has attempted to instigate my death at the hands of the Warriors."

"This is all speculation," Don Talone declared. "You can't prove Don Giorgio is involved."

The door suddenly opened.

Blade looked up at the man striding into the meeting room. His mind registered the cruel visage, the oily black hair, the brown eyes, and the black suit, and he intuitively realized the new arrival was Don Giorgio.

"Don Giorgio," Don Pucci said, confirming Blade's deduction. "You are early."

Don Giorgio scanned the room, his arrogant gaze lingering on the Warriors. "You've started the meeting without me?"

"You are the topic of our meeting," Don Pucci stated. "I'd hoped to settle matters before you arrived."

Don Giorgio stared at Don Pucci. "What kind of stunt are you trying to pull?"

"Why don't you take a seat?" Don Pucci suggested. "We would like to discuss the matter of a kidnapping with you."

"Is this a meeting of the Council or an interrogation?" Don Giorgio demanded testily.

"It is both," Don Pucci answered.

"I am insulted by your lack of courtesy," Don Giorgio said to Don Pucci. "I came over to your joint in good faith, with only six of my men, as required by our agreement. And now you say you want to grill me over some kidnapping?"

"We do not intend to grill you," Don Lansky said. "We merely want to ask a few questions."

"Why should I agree to this breech of etiquette," Don Giorgio snapped.

"If you have nothing to hide, I see no reason why you can't cooperate," Don Pucci stated.

Don Giorgio stared at each of the other Dons. "Are all of you in this together?"

"Don Pucci has made serious charges against you," Don Lansky offered placatingly. "We simply want to set the record straight."

"I refuse to be treated like one of the pezzonovante," Don Giorgio said disdainfully.

Embroiled in their dispute, accustomed to conducting their business in private amongst themselves, with their attention fully focused on another, they collectively disregarded the presence of the three Warriors. The last thing they expected was to have their conference interrupted by an outsider. So they were all the more disconcerted when a disruption abruptly occurred.

Helen walked up to the table and leveled her carbine at Don Giorgio. "Where's my daughter, you bastard!"

Don Giorgio stiffened. "Who the hell are you?"

"The name is Helen," she told him icily. "You kidnapped Mindy, my daughter. Where is she?"

"I did not kidnap your daughter, bitch!" Don Giorgio growled.

Helen shot him.

The single round caught Giorgio high on the right shoulder and spun him completely around. He doubled over, his left hand pressed against the wound, blood trickling over his fingers, his face contorted in savage rage.

Without exception, the other Dons were gawking at Giorgio, dumbfounded.

"Helen!" Blade said harshly, grabbing the Armalite barrel and pushing it upwards.

Just then the door opened and button men raced into the room, each with a handgun. Each of the Dons had arrived at the meeting with six soldiers, and now those trigger men flocked to their Dons while uneasily eyeing everyone else.

Don Pucci was the first to recover. "There will be no more shooting!" he commanded sternly.

Don Giorgio straightened and examined his wound.

"It's just a scratch," he said contemptuously. "The bitch can't shoot straight."

"If I'd wanted you dead," Helen assured him, "you'd be dead!"

Blade was expecting one of the soldiers to open up at any second. They were on edge, primed to kill. All it would take to initiate a blood bath was one wrong word or hasty action.

"I did not know she would do this," Don Pucci said to Giorgio.

"You allowed outsiders to attend a supreme Council meeting," Don Giorgio declared with a sneer. "And you can't even control them! Are you a Don or a windbag?"

"This regrettable incident was completely unforeseen," Don Pucci reiterated. "You have my apology."

"I don't want your apology!" Giorgio retorted. "I want this woman! It is my right!"

"She is here as my guest," Don Pucci said. "She is under my protection."

"Are you refusing to allow my right for revenge?" Don Giorgio demanded. "I am not armed, and she put a slug through me! I have the right to snuff her!"

A deep voice stabbed the air like a knife, drawing the scrutiny of everyone in the room to the giant in the black leather vest and the fatigue pants. "Like hell you do!"

Don Giorgio, strangely enough, grinned. "The mighty Blade speaks!" he said mockingly.

"So you know who I am," Blade remarked.

"I know all about you!" Don Giorgio boasted.

Blade leaned forward, resting his fists on the table. "Then you must know I'm a man of my word. And I'm giving you one hour to turn Mindy over to us, or we're coming after her."

"You're threatening me?" Giorgio rejoined furiously.

"No," Blade said softly. "I'm promising you. If Mindy isn't freed within an hour, we'll come get her."

Giorgio gazed at each of the Warriors. "All three of you?"

"They won't be alone," Don Pucci stated.

"Are you declaring war on me?" Don Giorgio snapped.

"I would rather not," Don Pucci said.

"I am not holding this Mindy," Giorgio declared. "How can you side with these scum against me?"

"I believe you kidnapped the girl," Don Pucci observed.

Giorgio's lips curled downwards. "Are you calling me a liar?"

There were several seconds of strained silence as the mobsters apprehensively waited for Don Pucci to respond. The fate of the seven Families hung in the balance. If he answered in the affirmative, each Don and every trigger man knew war was inevitable. And a war between any two Families would adversely affect all of them.

Don Pucci straightened in his wheelchair. "Yes. You are a lying peasant."

Don Giorgio took a menacing step forward. "Why, you worthless old shit! This is the final straw! I've tolerated your meddling long enough!"

Don Pucci's eyes narrowed. "Leave now, while you still can. I invited you here under an implied pledge of neutrality, and I won't violate the sanctity of the Council."

"You pompous old fart!" Giorgio declared. "Do you really think your Family is stronger than mine? You're in for a rude awakening."

"You have ten minutes to vacate the premises," Don Pucci said.

"What about the rest of you?" Don Giorgio asked, sweeping the other Dons with an expectant gaze. "Will you side with this fossil or me?"

None of the Dons responded.

"You'd better decide soon," Giorgio informed them. "I'll remember my friends when I'm on top, but I won't be so forgiving toward those who oppose me."

"We will not be intimidated," Don Marchese stated.

"Suit yourselves," Don Giorgio said. "I don't need you. I don't need any of you." He wheeled and stalked from the Council room, his soldiers on his heels.

"Now the shit hits the fan," Don Lansky remarked.

Don Pucci looked at Helen. "That was a very foolish thing you did. There was a remote chance I could have reasoned with Giorgio to return your daughter."

"You shouldn't have let him leave," Helen said in reproach. "I could have made him tell me where Mindy is being held."

Don Pucci faced his peers. "The harm has been done. There is no turning back. You must do as your conscience dictates. If you decide to remain neutral, I will understand."

"This is not our fight," Don Cuascut commented.

"In a sense, you're right," Don Pucci said. "Giorgio has been after me for years. This is a personal conflict as well as business. But keep one thing in mind. Giorgio is merciless. He wants absolute power. If he wins this war, what is to prevent him from trying to destroy your Families?" He paused. "Where do you stand?"

Don Causcut spoke first. "I want no part of it. My Family will be neutral."

"As you wish," Don Pucci said.

"Giorgio's Family is strong," Don Lansky noted. "I'd say the two of you are evenly matched. This war could drag out for months, even years. Our tourist trade would be crippled. Our economy would suffer. I do not like the idea of diminished coffers."

"You are with me then?" Don Pucci inquired hopefully.

"Respectfully, no," Don Lansky responded. "My Family will sit this out. This is between Giorgio and yourself. You must show the upstart the error of his ways. I will, however, provide whatever hardware and ammunition you may need."

"And you?" Don Pucci asked Don Marchese.

Marchese frowned. "I love you like a brother, Tony. You know that. And as a brother, I give you this advice. You must prove yourself by defeating Giorgio. He threw down the gauntlet and you accepted. Now you must prove yourself worthy of being the leader of our Council. So long as the war is strictly between Giorgio and yourself, I will not intervene one way or the other."

Don Siegel cleared his throat. "If the others are content to allow Giorgio and you to settle this, then so am I."

Don Pucci bowed his head. He did not want his friends to see his overwhelming disappointment.

"As for me," Don Talone added, "I'm not sticking my nose in where it doesn't belong. However, if Don Lansky is willing to supply arms to the Pucci Family, I can do no less for the Giorgio Family."

Don Pucci looked up at Don Talone. "Thank you for being honest. All of you should leave before the hostilities commence."

Without saying a word, the five Dons and their soldiers departed.

Don Pucci sighed and gazed at Blade. "The lines have been drawn, Warrior. For better or for worse, Don Giorgio and I will resolve our differences permanently."

"You're not alone in this," Blade said. "We're with you all the way."

Don Pucci smiled. "I appreciate the thought, but what can three Warriors do?"

"You've never seen us in action," Blade commented.

"Besides," Geronimo chimed in, "we have an ace in the hole. Or maybe I should refer to him as a wild card."

"Who is this wild card?" Pucci asked.

"Hickok."

CHAPTER SIXTEEN

Nadine's suite was sumptuously adorned. She closed the door behind them, flicked on the lights, and indicated a huge living room. "Make yourself at home."

Hickok sauntered into the living room, admiring the luxurious accommodations. "Wow! What do you do for a living? Rob banks?"

Nadine laughed and walked toward him. "Not quite. I'm a secretary."

"You must make a heap of dough," Hickok remarked, "if you can afford to live here."

"I don't live here, silly," Nadine said. "I'm renting the suite while I'm on vacation. I saved for a whole year to be able to stay here."

"You like to gamble?" Hickok commented.

Nadine winked at him. "I like excitement."

Hickok winked back. "Me too."

Nadine glanced at a door in the center of the right-hand wall. "Do you mind if I change into something a little more comfortable?"

"Suit yourself," Hickok said.

Nadine smiled and strolled to the door. "This will just take a minute or two. Don't go away!"

"I wouldn't think of it," Hickok assured her.

Nadine entered the next room and shut the door. "Stretch out on the sofa. I'll be right there," she called out.

"Okay," Hickok replied. Instead, he unslung the Henry and leaned it against a chair, then ran to the hall door and eased it open a crack.

A tail was in the corridor, approximately 20 feet away, leaning against the wall and staring moodily at the floor.

Hickok recognized the shadow. It was not the young mobster he'd spoken to in the casino. This was the *other* youngish mobster, the one in the brown suit, the one he'd seen in Don Giorgio's office. There must have been a changing of the guard. He closed the door and returned to the living room. As he was reclining on the sofa, Nadine emerged.

"Now I'm comfortable," she declared contentedly.

She was also almost naked. Hickok averted his eyes, gazing at a nearby chair. The red negligee she was wearing did an adequate job of covering her navel, but that was the only part of her anatomy it seemed to cover.

"What's wrong?" Nadine inquired, coming around the end of the sofa.

"Nothin'," Hickok mumbled.

"Don't tell me you're shy?" Nadine asked.

Hickok quickly sat up to give her room to sit. "Me? Shy? Not in a million years."

Nadine perched herself next to the gunman. "Do I embarrass you?"

"No," Hickok said. "But maybe you should put on a robe or something. You could catch your death from pneumonia."

Nadine laughed. "I'm fine. Believe me."

Hickok stood. "I believe you." He took a step away from the sofa, keeping his back to her. He held his right hand alongside his belt buckle and clenched his fist.

"You are shy!" Nadine exclaimed. She grabbed the

fringe of his buckskin shirt. "Come on. Have a seat. Let's get to know each other."

"I can't," Hickok said. "I'm hitched."

"So what if you're married?" Nadine commented. "It doesn't make a difference to me."

"Are you sure you want me to turn around?" Hickok inquired with the utmost civility.

Nadine tugged on his shirt. "Of course," he said.

"I should warn you," Hickok advised her. "I have a surprise for you."

"What kind of surprise?" Nadine inquired. She noticed the angle of his right arm and misconstrued his intent. "Oh, you naughty thing, you!" she declared, giggling. "I love kinky men!"

Hickok's brow furrowed. What the blazes was she talking about? "So you want my surprise?" he asked, wagging his fist.

Nadine caught the movement and tittered. "Give it to me!"

Hickok shrugged. "If you insist."

Nadine was grinning in lewd anticipation when he slugged her, his wiry form whipping around in a right arc, his right fist slamming into her jaw and flattening her on the sofa.

Hickok raised his fist for another blow, but the hooker was out cold, a rivulet of blood seeping out the left corner of her shapely mouth. "It may not make a difference to you, lady," he addressed the unconscious prostitute, "but it makes a world of difference to me. I'll never cheat on my missus."

Nadine groaned.

Hickok grabbed the Henry and dashed to the hall door again. He inched the door outwards until he could see the corridor.

The tail was gone!

Or was he?

What if the turkey had shifted positions? Hickok started to gingerly open the door wider, when suddenly the door was flung all the way open.

There stood the smirking mobster with a Detonics Combat Master MK VI in his right hand. "What are you up to, asshole?" he demanded.

"About six feet," Hickok replied.

"A smartass, huh?" the mobster said. "Up with your hands."

Hickok released the Henry and casually raised his arms.

"You didn't think I saw you before, did you?" the mobster mentioned. "But you don't pull one over on Ozzi that easily."

"Your handle is Ozzi?" Hickok queried.

"What if it is?" Ozzi peered over the gunfighter's left shoulder and spied Nadine on the sofa. "What did you do to her?"

"Nothin' much," Hickok said. "I tucked her in, is all."

"I knew you were up to no good," Ozzi stated. "Okay. You're coming with me."

"Where are we going?" Hickok questioned.

"To see Don Giorgio," Ozzi disclosed. "He went over to Pucci's joint but he should be back soon."

"Why don't we grab a bite to eat first?" Hickok suggested.

"And give you the chance to make a break?" Ozzi rejoined. "Not on your life. And keep those hands in the air. Don't try to touch those Colts. I've seen you in action, and I'm not taking any unnecessary risks. I've never seen anyone as fast as you."

Hickok grinned. "Thanks for the compliment."

"All Warriors must be morons," Ozzi muttered. He backed up several feet. "Let's go. Head for the stairwell at the end of this hall. And remember, if you lower your arms by a fraction, you're dead meat."

Hickok walked from the suite and turned in the direction Ozzi was indicating, to the right. The corridor was deserted. "Where is everybody?"

"Down in the casino," Ozzi replied. "The upper floors are like a tomb during the evening."

Hickok thoughtfully studied the green door ahead, debating whether to make his move there or wait for a better opportunity. There was a small window in the door at shoulder height.

"Stop!" Ozzi barked when they were six feet from the stairwell. "Stand facing the left wall."

Hickok obeyed.

Ozzi carefully moved past the Warrior and up to the door. He was about to push it open so he could enter the stairwell first. The Warrior might be tempted to swing the door into him, or use it as a shield while drawing the Colts. By going first, he thwarted both strategies. He detected motion on the other side of the door and glanced through the window.

Kenney was hurrying up the stairs, his countenance uncharacteristically grim. He disappeared a moment later.

What the hell?

For a few seconds Ozzi was mystified. Why was Kenney heading upstairs? Normally, Kenney would be conducting his daily casino rounds, inspecting all the tables and insuring everything was running smoothly. There was nothing upstairs of any interest. Except, of course, for Mindy.

Mindy!

A hard object unexpectedly touched Ozzi's left ear.

"Guess who?" Hickok quipped.

Ozzi gulped, his eyes on the stairwell.

"Let go of the hardware," Hickok directed, his right Colt pressed against the mobster's head. He grabbed the top of the Detonics pistol.

Ozzi released the weapon.

"Smart man," Hickok said. He slid the pistol under his belt. "Now let's mosey back to Nadine's room."

Ozzi slowly turned. His mind was racing with the implications of Kenney's presence in the stairwell. Kenney never varied his routine. Never. But the man was doing so now? Why? A queasy sensation developed in Ozzi's gut. "Wait!" he blurted.

"Quit stallin'," Hickok admonished.

Ozzi looked at the gunman. "Do you know Mindy?"

Hickok was instantly all attention. "Mindy? What

about her?"

"She's the reason you're here, right?" Ozzi inquired.

Hickok nodded. "How do you know about Mindy?"

Ozzi hesitated. What if he was wrong? The Don would never forgive him. But if he was right, then the Don must have sanctioned the killing. "Mindy is two floors up," he revealed. "I think she's in danger."

"What do you care?" Hickok asked suspiciously. "Is this your notion of a cockamamie trick?"

"No!" Ozzie responded. "I'm serious, man! She could be in danger."

"Take me to her," Hickok directed. If Mindy was really in danger, retrieving the Henry would have to wait. Every second counted.

Ozzi turned and opened the stairwell door. He took the stairs two at a stride.

Hickok stuck with the trigger man. He was puzzled by the mobster's evident sincerity, and he decided to go with his instincts. If Mindy was in the Palace, he intended to rescue her. And no passel of mangy city slickers was going to stand in his way!

Ozzi passed the landing for the ninth floor.

Hickok drew his left Colt.

As the landing for the tenth floor loomed overhead, Ozzi slowed slightly. What if he was making a fool of himself? What if Kenney was just checking on Mindy's welfare? He was behaving rashly, and a wiseguy needed a cool head at all times. What had Don Giorgio said in Minnesota? "If you blow your cool, you're a fool." His best bet was to confirm Mindy was okay on the sly, a task he could not perform with the Warrior in tow. No sooner did the realization dawn upon him than he threw himself backwards, hoping to catch the gunman unawares.

He nearly succeeded.

Hickok's lightning reflexes served him in good stead. He dodged to the left to avoid the hit man's hurtling body, but Ozzi grabbed his right arm and yanked, causing him to lose his balance and to topple backwards.

The pair tumbled down the stairwell for eight feet.

Hickok's head smacked onto the edge of one of the

concrete steps, and he wound up on his left side, dazed. He saw Ozzi come out of a roll and dive toward him, and he managed to lash out with his right foot and kick the button man in the face.

Ozzi was knocked for a loop. He landed on his back, four steps below the Warrior.

Hickok surged erect as Ozzi was rising. He took a stride and slammed the barrel of his right Python across the mobster's mouth.

Ozzi, staggered, reeled.

Hickok closed in, battering the hit man again and again. First the left Colt, then the right, then the left once more.

Ozzi, his mouth and chin a bloody, pulpy mess, sank to his knees, then collapsed.

Hickok was tempted to plug the varmint, but the shot might attract other gangsters. He holstered the Colts and glanced up the stairwell. Was Mindy really in the building, or had Ozzi fabricated the story to augment his chances of turning the tide? Hickok knew he couldn't afford to leave without verifying whether Mindy was in the Palace, whether she actually was on the tenth floor.

He jogged up the stairs.

If Ozzi had been right about everyone being down in the casino, finding an alternate exit from the Palace should be a piece of cake. A side door would suffice, or a window close to the ground.

Hickok reached the tenth floor landing and halted, peering through the window in the door.

The corridor was vacant.

Warily, his ears straining, Hickok opened the door and stepped into the hallway. He advanced slowly until he came abreast of the nearest door on the right. His right hand closed on the doorknob.

The danged thing was locked!

Hickok frowned as he surveyed the corridor. There were over a dozen rooms. Which one was Mindy in? He walked to the next door, which was on the left, and touched the knob.

A piercing, terrified scream abruptly shattered the stillness.

CHAPTER SEVENTEEN

"How did you persuade all of your customers to leave so quickly?" Blade asked.

"Would you want to be caught in the middle of a war?" Don Pucci rejoined.

Blade grinned. "I see your point."

They were in the center of the casino, watching the preparations being made by the Don's soldiers. Over three dozen armed trigger men were industriously piling furniture and wooden crates several feet from the ten glass doors, erecting a makeshift wall.

Mario approached. "The calls have all been made," he announced. "All the troops will be here within the hour."

"Weapons?" Don Pucci queried.

"All the weapons and explosives are being brought up from downstairs," Mario replied.

"What if Giorgio attacks before you're ready for him?" Blade inquired.

"He won't attack," the Don responded.

"Why not?"

"Giorgio is scum, but he's not stupid," Don Pucci said.

"Right now he's doing the same thing I'm doing, fortifying his casino and calling in his button men. This will be a war of attrition." He paused. "Constructing his casino next to mine was a stroke of genius."

"How so?" Blade probed.

"Years ago, Giorgio and I were on friendly terms. His ambition was not so obvious, but he was planning ahead, even then," Don Pucci detailed. "He asked to build his casino across the boulevard, and I assented. Now his reasons are obvious. No one will be able to enter or leave by the front doors. Our business will grind to a halt, and our financial reserves will be severely depleted the longer the war continues. If I run out of funds, I will be seriously weakened. Money talks in this town. Giorgio is in a position to keep tabs on every activity around the casino."

"But it works both ways," Blade noted. "And you'll still have the rear exits you can use."

"Unless Giorgio tries to surround the Golden Crown, to cut it off from the rest of the city," Don Pucci said. "Our provisions will not last indefinitely."

"Will you take the offensive?" Blade questioned.

"Not until I can find a weak link in Giorgio's defenses," Don Pucci responded.

Blade looked over his right shoulder at Geronimo and Helen.

Geronimo nodded.

"What if we were to weaken his defenses for you?" Blade asked, staring at the Don.

Pucci studied the giant for a moment. "I can't ask you to do that."

"Mindy and Hickok are in the Palace," Blade said. "We must go after them."

"You'll be cut down before you cross the boulevard," Don Pucci commented.

"Perhaps," Blade stated. "But if we can punch a hole in his defenses before he's ready, if we can keep him occupied, you'd have the advantage you need."

"Hmmmm," Don Pucci said thoughtfully. "Attack him now, before he's ready, before he has the opportunity to call in all of his soldiers? He'd never expect a direct assault now, because he undoubtedly assumes I'm too busy mobilizing my forces." He grinned. "It could work."

Blade looked at Mario. "You mentioned explosives. What kind do you have?"

"Name it, we have it," Mario replied. "Dynamite, grenades, plastic explosives."

"Any smoke bombs?" Blade asked.

Mario nodded. "A crate or two."

"We'll need a crate of smoke bombs and four grenades apiece," Blade stated.

Mario looked at Don Pucci, who nodded curtly. Mario hastened off.

"How do you propose to proceed?" Pucci queried the giant.

"We'll go in first," Blade said. "Hold back your men for several minutes. We want Giorgio totally unprepared for your attack. If he's involved with fighting us, he won't notice our ruse until it's too late."

"You take great risks, my friend," Don Pucci commented.

"Nothing ventured, nothing gained," Blade philosophized.

"I just pray that Mindy is still alive," Helen remarked anxiously.

"And Hickok," Geronimo added.

Blade stared at the Don. "If Giorgio loses, what happens to his Family?"

"They will be absorbed into my Family," Don Pucci answered. "They will owe their allegiance to me."

"You won't conduct reprisals?" Blade inquired.

"No. Why should I? Senseless reprisals are a waste," Don Pucci said. "The easiest way to kill a snake is to cut off its head, not chop its body into little pieces."

"With Giorgio's Family combined with your own," Blade noted, "you'll be the undisputable leader in Vegas. No one else will challenge you."

"I hope you are right," Pucci said. "But you never know. There is always someone who believes the grass is greener on the other side of the fence."

The makeshift wall was six feet high, and the mobsters had ceased piling furniture and were passing out machine guns.

Mario returned, attended by four men carrying two heavy crates. The men deposited the crates near the Warriors.

"Here you go," Mario said. "A crate of smoke bombs and a crate of grenades. Take whatever you need." He glanced at the men. "Open them."

One of the men departed, only to return moments later with a crowbar. The quartet applied themselves to prying the tops off.

"We'll need some assistance from you to get across the boulevard," Blade mentioned to the Don.

"Anything you want, you get," Don Pucci declared.

"I need a car," Blade detailed. "Can you have one running behind your casino within five minutes?"

Don Pucci snapped his fingers and Mario ran toward the rear of the casino.

"Will Don Giorgio have men watching the back?" Blade inquired.

"He might, but I doubt it," Pucci responded. "He hasn't had the time to get all his troops in place."

"What about the boulevard and the side streets? Will they be cordoned off?" Blade needed to know.

"No," Pucci said. "No one in their right mind will come near either casino. The Enforcers will keep everyone away from both joints."

"Are the Enforcers your men?" Blade questioned.

"The Enforcers are selected from every Family," Don Pucci revealed. "They take an oath of neutrality and serve for one year. After their duty, they return to their Family."

"So they won't take a part in this conflict?" Blade remarked.

"No," Don Pucci said. "Neither will the other Dons, if they stick by their word."

"Okay, then," Blade stated. "We will circle around the

Golden Crown and approach the Palace on the boulevard. When you hear a single shot, have a dozen of your men hurl smoke bombs out to the middle of the boulevard. We'll do the rest."

The tops were off the crates.

Blade moved to the crate of grenades and selected four, stuffing two into each front pocket. "Each of you take four," he instructed Geronimo and Helen.

Geronimo hefted one of the grenades. "I just hope this doesn't accidentally go off in my pants. My wife would be terribly disappointed."

"I hope I get to cram one of these down Giorgio's throat!" Helen said angrily.

Mario was running toward them. "The car is all set. It's an antique Buick, built like a tank."

"Thanks," Blade said. He looked at the Don and extended his right hand.

The Don, somewhat surprised, took the huge hand in his own.

"I want your word," Blade declared. "If something should happen to me, my friends must be permitted to leave Vegas unharmed, no matter what else happens."

Don Pucci appeared hurt by the implication. "Need you ask?"

"No, I guess not," Blade said. He squeezed the Don's hand and let go.

"Let's go find that ding-a-ling in buckskins," Geronimo remarked.

"May God be with you," the Don said to Blade. "Oh! I almost forgot. It's important that you know Giorgio lives on the third floor."

"Come with me," Mario directed. He turned and jogged in the direction of a door on the left-hand side of the rear wall.

Blade kept pace with the man in white, Geronimo and Helen on his heels.

Behind them, Don Pucci was barking orders.

They crossed the casino, following Mario down a tiled corridor until they came to an enormous kitchen with white walls and sparkling utensils. Once through the kitchen, they traversed another hallway and exited the building by way of a red door. Before them was a sprawling parking lot filled with vehicles. Armed mobsters ringed the rear of the casino. Ten yards from the door was a dark blue Buick, the engine idling, three hit men standing near the grill.

"There's your car," Mario said.

They ran to the Buick.

One of the men near the grill looked at the Warriors, then at the car. "This is mine," he said sadly. "She's an antique. I've spent every spare penny I've earned to fix her up."

Mario smacked the front fender. "It's as solid as they come."

Blade opened the driver's door and slid in. The front seat was somewhat cramped for a man of his size. All the windows were down.

Geronimo and Helen walked to the other side. Helen climbed into the rear and Geronimo took the passenger side, resting the Browning barrel on the dash.

"Good luck," Mario offered, and hurried inside.

Blade closed his door and gripped the wheel.

The three mobsters had moved to one side.

"Try to keep her in one piece," the owner called sorrowfully. He looked like he was about to cry.

"I'll try," Blade said, and shifted into drive. He drove toward an exit on the northern boundary of the parking lot.

"Do you have a plan?" Geronimo asked.

"We'll use the Buick to get inside the Palace," Blade said. "Once we're there, we'll unload the grenades. After that, we wing it."

"I'm going to find Mindy," Helen vowed. "And I'll kill anyone who stands in my way."

"I hope Hickok and Mindy are okay," Geronimo commented.

"Check your weapons," Blade advised. He took a right at the exit and cruised toward the boulevard.

"Funny," Helen remarked. "I'm not nervous at all. I thought I'd have butterflies by now."

"You can have some of mine," Geronimo offered.

Blade was driving at five miles an hour. He surveyed the side street, pleased to note there wasn't a single soul anywhere. He did not want innocent bystanders harmed.

The boulevard appeared ahead.

Blade slowed until the Buick was scarcely moving. "We have to time this just right. Giorgio's men can't spot us before we reach the corner because the Golden Crown blocks their view. Once we reach the corner, they're bound to cut loose unless Pucci's men come through." He glanced at Geronimo. "When I give the word, fire one shot."

Geronimo drew his Arminius from its shoulder holster under his right arm. He cocked the revolver and poked the gun out of the window. "Ready."

Blade coasted to a stop 30 feet from the intersection. He unslung the Commando and placed the machine gun on his lap.

"I haven't seen any traffic on the boulevard," Helen mentioned.

"There shouldn't be any," Blade said. He stared at her, then Geronimo. "Take care of yourselves. And keep your eyes peeled for Hickok and Mindy."

"Say, Blade," Helen began.

"What?"

"If I don't make it, make sure Mindy reaches the Home," Helen said.

"You'll make it," Blade told her. He gazed at the boulevard and took a deep breath. "Give the signal."

Geronimo fired once.

Blade mentally counted to ten. Pucci's men should be tossing the smoke bombs into the boulevard. The smoke would disperse rapidly, enshrouding the boulevard between the two casinos in a gray haze. He was on eight when he heard the crackle of gunfire. That would be Giorgio's soldiers, belatedly firing at Pucci's men with the smoke bombs.

Nine.

Ten.

Blade tramped on the accelerator and the antique Buick surged forward. He took a sharp right at the intersection, the tires squealing, and angled the car toward the Palace. As expected, a cloaking cloud of smoke enveloped the boulevard. For several seconds he couldn't see a thing. He could only hope he was traveling in the right direction. Twice the Buick was unexpectedly jolted as it struck unseen objects.

Bodies?

The Buick bounced and bucked as it hit yet a third obstacle, and then the smoke was thinning.

Blade's hands inadvertently tightened on the steering wheel. They were on the short flight of cement steps leading up to the Palace's seven glass doors! "We're going to hit!" he cried, keeping the accelerator on the floor.

Faces were visible on the other side of the doors, astonished visages of shocked mobsters.

Blade ducked his head to spare his eyes from the flying glass.

With a resounding, thunderous crash, the Buick rammed into the center of the row of glass doors. The glass shattered, the metal frames buckling like so much paper. Beyond the doors was a hastily constructed wall of furniture and boxes similar to the barrier Don Pucci's men had erected in the Golden Crown. Its momentum hardly impeded by the doors, its engine roaring, the Buick plowed into the barricade, sending chairs and boxes and busted pieces of furniture in every direction. Several mobsters were hit by the grill and battered aside. Curses, shouts, and screams arose. And still the Buick hurtled onward.

Blade spied a group of hit men to the left and slewed the Buick toward them. They frantically attempted to evade the dreadnought, but he ruthlessly mowed them down.

Guns started firing, peppering the Buick's thick frame.

Fifteen yards off were rows of slot machines.

Blade slammed on the brakes. The Buick screeched to a jarring halt, its rear end whipping around and colliding with one of the slot machines, its front end facing the incensed mobsters. "Out!" he shouted, and shoved his door open.

The Buick's windshield dissolved in a spray of lead.

Blade vaulted from the car, rolling on his left shoulder and rising in a crouch with the Commando leveled. He squeezed the trigger, firing a burst into a charging cluster of hit men. Scrambling backwards, he reached the slot machines and ducked behind the nearest one.

Geronimo and Helen were coming around the passenger side, shooting on the run.

Blade stood, providing covering fire.

"Get them!" someone was bellowing. "Nail those sons of bitches!"

Helen took cover in back of a slot machine.

Geronimo blasted the Browning one more time, then dived for shelter.

Shots were thudding into the slot machines.

Giorgio's trigger men were assembling for a mass charge.

"Grenades!" Blade yelled, reaching into his right front pocket. He extracted one of his grenades and crouched close to the floor.

Geronimo and Helen did likewise.

Blade peeked around the edge of the slot machine. The mobsters were just starting forward, about 30 of them. "On the count of three!" he directed.

The slot machines were being struck again and again.

"Two."

There was a loud, defiant whoop from the hit men as they charged the slots.

"Three."

As one, the Warriors pulled the pins on their grenades and rose, their arms already sweeping back, then arcing around. The grenades sailed over the Buick, perfectly thrown, landing on the carpet in front of the onrushing mobsters and rolling under their pumping legs.

Blade, Geronimo, and Helen flattened.

The three concussions combined to produce an awesome

shock wave, and the floor seemed to heave upward and settle down again.

Bits of flesh and chunks of bodies were blown across the room. Several legs rained to the carpet.

"Oh me!" Blade commanded, heaving erect and racing for the rear of the casino. He wanted to draw Giorgio's men away from the front entrance. Two hit men appeared and he killed them both.

Geronimo and Helen were pouring a lethal hail of lead into any and all targets.

Blade noticed a door to his left. He sprinted toward it.

A mobster popped up from behind a table ten feet to the right, a shotgun in his hands, aiming at the giant.

Blade started to whirl, knowing he would be too late, expecting to feel the buckshot tearing through his body.

Helen saved him. Her carbine boomed, and the mobster, hit in the face, was flung backwards.

Blade dashed to the door. He wrenched on the knob and pulled it wide, intending to seek temporary sanctuary in the corridor beyond.

A dozen or so trigger men were rushing down the hall toward the door, coming to the aid of their colleagues.

"Hey! Look!" one of them shouted. "Who's he?"

Blade spun, desperately seeking somewhere they could defend against the mobsters.

Another group of soldiers was storming across the casino.

They were trapped!

CHAPTER EIGHTEEN

Hickok glanced to the right, in the direction of the scream. Was that Mindy? He raced along the corridor, hoping the scream would be repeated so he could pinpoint the room.

It was.

A second, subdued shriek punctuated the hall, emanating from a room to the right.

Hickok reached the door in two bounds. He tried to twist the knob, but the door was locked.

So what!

Hickok took a step back, then kicked, planting his right foot next to the doorknob.

The door held firm.

Frowning, Hickok struck with his foot twice more, and on the second kick there was a splintering crunch and the doorframe split from the base to the top. He tensed his left shoulder and slammed into the center of the door. He was elated when it swiveled inward, the lock dangling from only one screw.

Dear Spirit!

Hickok's elation turned to dismay at the sight he beheld: Kenney was straddling Mindy on a bed, striving to choke the life from her with a ragged strip of yellow bedspread.

Mindy was feebly swatting at Kenney's arms.

Kenney glanced up in shock at the Warrior. He released his grip and tried to reach a pistol under his left arm.

Hickok's reaction was instantaneous. He drew his right Colt and snapped off a shot.

The slug ripped through Kenney's right eye and out the rear of his head, the impact twisting his body to the right and knocking him to the floor.

"Mindy!" Hickok exclaimed, running to the bed and holstering his Colt.

Mindy stared at the Warrior in transparent relief. She clawed at the strip of bedspread, gasping for air.

Hickok swiftly removed the crude garrote.

"Hickok!" Mindy exclaimed, her voice raspy and hoarse. She was up and hugging him in the twinkling of an eye.

Hickok embraced her awkwardly for a moment. "There, there," he consoled her, feeling her tremble in his arms. "You're okay. You're safe. Everything is hunky-dory."

Mindy placed her face in the crook of his neck. Moist tears touched his skin. "Oh, Hickok!" she gasped.

"That's my handle. Don't wear it out," he said light-heartedly.

"Hickok!" Mindy stated again, as if his name was a tonic to her tortured emotions.

"We can't stay here," Hickok advised her.

"I'm scared," Mindy blurted. "That man almost killed me!"

"His killin' days are over," Hickok assured her.

Mindy stepped back, courageously composing herself. "Who else is with you?"

"Blade, some ornery Injun with a penchant for bull-slingin', and your mom," Hickok disclosed.

Mindy brightened. "My mom is here!"

"In the Golden Crown, across the street," Hickok said.

"We've got to find them."

Mindy rubbed her tender neck, taking deep breaths. "Give me a minute. I feel weak."

"That's to be expected," Hickok remarked, glancing at the doorway. "We really must skedaddle."

"In a second," she said. "You know, it's funny. I used to occasionally view being a Weaver at the Home as a dull vocation. But no more! I'll never gripe about my lot in life again! From now on, I—"

"Save it," Hickok said, cutting her off. He took hold of her right hand and walked toward the corridor. "I'm tickled pink that you've found your niche in life. I truly am. But this isn't the time or place for yakkin' about it. We've got to make tracks."

"Sorry," Mindy mumbled. "I'm just so happy! I feel like I could walk on air."

"I wish we could walk on air," Hickok commented. "It'd make gettin' out of here a lot easier." He stopped in the center of the hallway and gazed in both directions.

No mobsters were in sight.

"Maybe we lucked out," Hickok observed. "Maybe no one heard my shot."

"Which way?" Mindy inquired.

"The stairwell," Hickok suggested, retracing his steps. Once they were in the stairwell, he increased his pace.

"Where does this lead?" Mindy questioned.

"Whisper," he whispered.

"Where does this lead?" Mindy repeated in a hushed voice.

"Down," Hickok stated the obvious. "There might be an exit door at the bottom."

"I can't wait to see my mother again," Mindy mentioned.

Hickok abruptly halted.

"What is it?" Mindy asked apprehensively.

Hickok stared at the steps in perplexity. "The polecat is gone!" He peered over the railing.

"What polecat?" Mindy inquired.

"Later," Hickok said. They descended to the eighth

floor. He told her to wait, entered the hall, and returned in ten seconds with a rifle slung across his back. "My Henry," he explained, taking her hand once more. Down they went.

From far below came the muffled, yet unmistakable, report of an explosion. They heard the faint sound of gunfire.

"What's going on?" Mindy questioned.

"I wish I knew," Hickok muttered. He hastened ever lower, pondering the ramifications of the conflict being waged. From the sound of things, a full-fledged war had erupted. But who would be attacking Don Giorgio? And why? His friends must have come looking for him, and somehow managed to get into hot water. Leave it to those dummies to get into trouble when he had everything under control!

The noise of the shooting, intermixed with shouting and screams, grew louder and louder.

They passed landing after landing until they were between the fourth floor and the third, not ten feet from the landing door, which abruptly opened.

Hickok drew Mindy back against the stairwell wall. Her fingernails bit into the palm of his hand.

Six mobsters appeared and promptly descended the stairs. None of them bothered to look upward.

"Whew!" Mindy exclaimed. "That was close!"

"Come on." Hickok stepped down to the landing. He released Mindy's hand and cautiously approached the door. Don Giorgio's suite was on this floor. He looked through the window, verifying the hallway was vacant. "Don Giorgio was responsible for kidnapping you, wasn't he?"

"Yes," Mindy said.

"No one else?" Hickok asked.

"Just Giorgio's goons," Mindy replied. "Why?"

"Did you ever hear of a Don Pucci?" Hickok inquired.

"I heard the name mentioned," Mindy answered. "But I never met him. I was under the impression that Giorgio and Pucci are not on the best of terms."

Hickok nodded. "Everything is fallin' into place. I want you to stick close to me."

"I'm not about to wander off," Mindy promised.

"Walk directly behind me," Hickok instructed her. "If one of us is going to take a slug, I'd rather it be me."

"What do you mean by take a slug?" Mindy responded nervously.

Hickok didn't reply. He yanked the door wide and boldly proceeded along the corridor.

Mindy was about to inquire about the reason for leaving the stairwell, when a door ahead opened and two hit men emerged. They both toted machine guns, and their eyes widened as they saw the Warrior. She quickly stepped behind Hickok, but peeked around his right shoulder.

"Who are you?" one of the button men demanded.

"Where is Giorgio?" Hickok rejoined, his arms draped at his sides.

"Who the hell wants to know?" snapped the mobster.

"His executioner," Hickok replied.

The button men tried to bring their machine guns into play.

Mindy was opening her mouth to screech in mortal terror, momentarily forgetting who she was with and overlooking his reputation, certain they were both about to be shot.

But it was the other way around.

She glimpsed a blurred streak as Hickok pulled his revolvers and fired, the twin shots deafening in the corridor.

Each mobster was hit in the face just above the nose. Each one stumbled backwards and toppled over.

Hickok suddenly began walking quite rapidly toward the door at the end of the hall.

Mindy dogged him like a shadow.

A burly mobster stepped from a room on the left, a pistol in his right hand.

Hickok plugged him between the eyes, then walked even faster then before.

Mindy detected an urgency in his movements. She

marveled at the shootings she had witnessed. He had slain four men in twice as many minutes, and she wondered if she would see him kill more.

She did.

They were eight feet from the door at the end of the hall when it swung inward, framing a trigger man with a shotgun in the doorway.

Hickok shot him in the forehead.

Mindy was within an inch of the Warrior's back, craning her neck to look over his right shoulder. She intuitively sensed she was about to witness an exploit few Family members had been privileged to observe at close quarters: Hickok in action. She had heard stories of his deeds during the war against the Doktor and elsewhere, but she had never personally been an eyewitness to his prowess.

Now she was.

Hickok went through the doorway at a brisk clip, striding over the corpse blocking the door.

Mindy found herself in a large room containing a lot of chairs. On the other side of the room was a closed door, and the Warrior stalked up to it and flung it open.

A pair of trigger men were running toward them. One was armed with a machine gun, the other a pistol.

Hickok went for the most dangerous adversary first, the man with the machine gun. His right Colt cracked, and the trigger man reacted like he had been pounded in the head by an invisible sledge hammer; the mobster flipped backward onto a desk.

But even as Hickok had fired, so had the trigger man with the pistol.

Mindy saw Hickok's left shoulder jerk, and something tugged at her red hair. With a start, she realized the Warrior had been hit!

Hickok's left Python boomed, and the second mobster sprouted an extra nostril and pitched forward.

Mindy went to touch Hickok, to ask if he was okay, but he was pressing toward yet another door in their path. He was reaching for the doorknob when he did a very strange thing; he unexpectedly swept his left arm around, forcing her away from the shut door.

Not a second too soon.

The door was rocked by a machine-gun burst, the slugs bursting the wood outwards and crashing into the walls and furniture surrounding them.

Mindy flinched, covering her face with her right arm.

As abruptly as it began, the firing ceased.

And Hickok moved. He reached the door in a leaping stride and rammed his right foot into the lower half. The ravaged door swiveled inward.

Mindy, remembering his instructions to stay near him always, darted behind him in time to see a heavyset man fumbling with a mechanism on the large machine gun he was holding. He looked up, staring calmly at the Warrior, and he actually grinned.

"Wouldn't you know it," he commented pensively. "The damn thing jammed."

"Better luck next time," Hickok said, and his left Colt blasted.

The heavyset mobster stiffened as his left eye vanished and the rear of his cranium exploded, showering hair and flesh all over the thick carpet. He sagged to his knees, then fell forward.

Hickok strode into the huge chamber, glancing from left to right. "Blast!" he fumed. "Giorgio isn't here."

"But I am," said a mocking voice behind them.

Mindy, horrified, recognizing the voice, whirled.

There he was, covered with blood from his eyebrows to his waist, his nose twisted to the left, his lips split and several teeth broken, his chin and cheeks puffy and marked by welts, a machine gun in his hands, a furious gleam in his eyes.

"Ozzi!" Mindy cried.

Ozzi swept the machine-gun barrel to within a hairsbreadth of her nose. "Yes! Ozzi!"

Hickok had turned at the sound of Ozzi's voice, but his line of fire had been obstructed by Mindy. He shifted to the right.

"Don't even think it!" Ozzi growled, his finger

quivering on the trigger. "You do, and she's worm meat!"

Hickok frowned and tilted the Python barrels up at the ceiling.

"That's real smart," Ozzi said. "Now drop the revolvers!"

Hickok never hesitated. He knew he could drill Ozzi before the hit man squeezed the machine gun's trigger, and he also knew Ozzi's finger might tighten on the trigger in a reflexive death spasm. Either way, Mindy would die. Ozzi was holding a fully automatic Bushmaster.

The Colts fell to the carpet.

Ozzi beamed maliciously. "Now the Detonics and the rifle."

Hickok had forgotten about the pistol tucked under his belt. He slowly eased it loose and let go, then placed the Henry on the floor.

Ozzi glared at the Warrior, then Mindy. "Did you really think you'd get away from me?"

Mindy didn't answer.

Ozzi's eyes narrowed. "You're not so clever, bitch! I finally figured out why you turned down my marriage proposal."

Despite her revulsion and fear, Mindy responded. "Why?"

"Because you've got the hots for him," Ozzi said, leering.

"I do not!" Mindy declared, insulted at the insinuation.

Ozzi's lips curled away from his teeth. He resembled a rabid dog about to bite. "Don't lie to me! I know better!"

"You wouldn't know the truth if you tripped over it," Hickok said, hoping to draw some of the heat from Mindy.

Ozzi made a snarling noise and motioned to the right with the machine gun. "Get over there!" he barked at Mindy. "Move!"

Mindy shuffled several feet to the right.

Ozzi sneered at the Warrior. "Turn around!"

Hickok balked.

"Do it, or I'll shoot the bitch!" Ozzi roared.

Reluctantly, Hickok turned completely around.

Ozzi stepped over to the gunman and savagely rammed the barrel of his weapon into the Warrior's lower back.

Hickok gasped and clutched at the spot, lanced with agony.

Cackling, Ozzi pounded the Bushmaster across the gunfighter's head.

Hickok lurched forward, trying to pivot to protect himself.

With a cruel, primal, delight, Ozzi struck the Warrior on the left temple twice in succession.

Blood sprayed from Hickok's temple and he dropped onto his right knee, still struggling, striving to reach the mobster.

Ozzi slammed the Bushmaster's stock into the side of the Warrior's head, and Hickok finally went down. Laughing, Ozzi rotated toward Mindy. "Now it's your turn, bitch! You're going to suffer for what I've been through!"

Mindy retreated a step, panic welling within her.

"I owe you!" Ozzi declared. He gestured menacingly with the machine gun. "You'll be groveling at my feet before I'm through."

"Let us go!" Mindy pleaded. "Please!"

"Please!" Ozzi said, imitating the whine in her tone. "Kiss the world good-bye, scuzz!" He aimed at her chest.

"Wait!" commanded a new voice.

Mindy glanced at the doorway and nearly fainted. Just when she thought the situation couldn't possibly become any worse, it did.

Don Giorgio and Sacks had arrived!

CHAPTER NINETEEN

"Grenades!" Blade bellowed, tugging the second grenade from his pocket and pulling the pin as slugs smacked into the walls around him. He heaved the grenade into the corridor and dove for the floor.

Geronimo and Helen were just releasing their grenades at the group charging across the casino. Geronimo grunted and twisted to the right, then flattened. Helen followed suit.

The grenade in the corridor detonated first, and the cries of torment from the maimed and dying arose an instant later.

At the sight of the two grenades arching their way, the group in the casino frantically endeavored to disperse. They bumped into one another in their frenzy to escape the hurtling doom, and they were largely unsuccessful. A mere handful survived. The grenades went off in their midst— *Whomp! Whomp!*—and literally blew them to shredded pieces.

Blade crawled into the corridor, the Commando in front of him. Five or six trigger men were alive and closing. He fired, sweeping the Commando from side to side, stopping the mobsters with a withering wall of lead. As the last one fell, he jumped to his feet. "Oh me!"

Helen darted into the corridor.

Geronimo joined them, his right hand pressed against his side, grimacing. "I'm hit," he mentioned.

"How bad?" Blade asked.

"It creased my side," Geronimo said. "I can manage. Let's move!"

Blade raced for a door at the far end of the hallway. He could hear his companions pounding after him. They wound past the bodies of the dead mobsters, past unattached, ruptured limbs and contorted torsos. Once he almost slipped in a puddle of gore. Some of the trigger men were groaning piteously.

One of the soldiers, a man with a gaping hole in his abdomen, clutched at Helen's legs. She tripped, righted herself, and shot him in the mouth.

Blade was beginning to believe they would reach the door without further incident, but he was wrong. They were less than 15 feet from their goal when gunfire broke out to their rear.

The Warriors whirled, dropping to their knees.

Seven mobsters from the casino were in hot pursuit, firing as they ran.

Geronimo went prone, sighting the Browning and squeezing the trigger with a practiced economy of movement, the BAR thundering.

The leader of the pursuing pack dropped.

Helen lifted the Armalite and aimed at the next mobster. His life was momentarily spared when the carbine clicked instead of discharging. "Empty!" she cried, discarding the Armalite and drawing her .45-caliber Caspians. She fired both automatics simultaneously, and her original target tumbled to the floor.

Blade removed his third grenade, slipping it from his left front pocket and yanking on the pin. He spied one of the mobsters doing the same thing, and he tossed his before Giorgio's man could let fly. "Grenade!" he yelled, and sprawled onto his stomach.

The five remaining gangsters were virtually obliterated. They were packed together when both grenades exploded, one after the other. The corridor heaved and shook, plaster falling from the ceiling, dust permeating the air and obscuring the grisly remnants of the mobsters.

Blade was up and jogging to the door before the dust could settle. He distinctly heard shots from the casino, and he wondered if Don Pucci's men were assaulting the Palace. He reached the door and wrenched it wide, finding a stairwell on the other side.

Geronimo and Helen ran to the door. Geronimo was reloading the Browning. Helen had replaced the Caspians and was slapping a fresh clip into the Armalite.

"Ready?" Blade queried.

They nodded grimly.

Blade darted into the stairwell without bothering to establish whether Giorgio's men were already there, and he immediately regretted his foolhardiness.

Six well-armed trigger men were rounding a bend in the stairs above, halfway between the doorway and the next landing. They opened up the second they saw him.

Blade hit the floor and rolled alongside the stairs, effectively screening his body from view from above.

Geronimo and Helen, still in the corridor, provided covering fire.

The mobsters were compelled to retreat up the stairs to the landing.

All firing abruptly stopped.

Blade risked a hasty glance upward. The trigger men were not in sight. Were they hiding on the landing, waiting for the Warriors to ascend, or had they fled? Giorgio's men did not impress him as the craven type.

A minute elapsed.

Blade rose to a crouch and moved to the base of the stairs, his eyes on the landing.

Nothing.

Geronimo and Helen were waiting at the doorway, one on either side.

With his Commando angled upward, Blade cautiously advanced to the halfway point.

Still nothing.

Blade hesitated, chafing at the delay. Reaching the third floor swiftly was imperative. Don Giorgio's termination was essential if Don Pucci was to triumph. Every second the Warriors dallied increased the likelihood of Giorgio escaping.

Giorgio must *not* get away!

His lips a compressed line, Blade moved higher. In four strides he could see the landing clearly.

The mobsters were gone.

Geronimo and Helen were waiting at the bottom of the steps.

Blade motioned for them to join him, and while they climbed the steps he inserted a new magazine into the Commando, even though the one he replaced still contained over a dozen rounds.

"Where did they go?" Geronimo whispered.

"Beats me," Blade replied quietly.

"Do you hear all the gunshots coming from the casino?" Helen inquired.

Blade nodded. "Don Pucci's men, I bet. Which means Giorgio's soldiers in the casino will be preoccupied for a while. There could be more of his trigger men scattered throughout the building. If there are any on this next floor, I don't care. We'll leave them for Pucci's men to mop up. I say we're going directly to the third floor. Odds are, that's where we'll find Giorgio."

"Then what are we waiting for?" Helen asked sharply. "I want to get my hands on that bastard!"

"Let's go." Blade took off up the stairwell, alertly scanning the stairs overhead for any sign of the six trigger men. They passed the landing and kept going, and only when they were almost to the next bend did he realize his blatant error.

The six mobsters had not fled. They had gone into the corridor and crouched low against the walls, waiting for their foes to open the landing door so they could gun the giant and the other two down. Their ambush was thwarted when the three continued upward, but the mobsters were equally pleased. They simply waited for the giant, the woman, and the Indian to climb a little higher, and without any warning the trigger men spilled onto the landing and blasted away.

Blade heard the landing door opening, and he tried to spin, knowing he had committed a grave mistake. Geronimo and Helen were also in motion, but they were all too late.

All three Warriors were hit.

Blade felt a searing, burning sensation in his right side. He winced, forcing his mind to disregard the pain as he returned the mobsters' fire.

Geronimo took a slug in the left thigh. He stumbled backwards and fell, landing on his right side. Twisting, he brought the Browning to bear and squeezed the trigger.

Helen, her body at an angle, trying to reach the cover of the bend as she sighted on the trigger men, was struck twice. The first shot dug a bloody furrow in her right cheek. The second shot tore through her right shoulder just under the bone. She was bowled over by the impact, stunned for several seconds.

Blade saw two of the trigger men go down. The remainder ducked into the corridor. He could guess their strategy; they would regroup and reload, and in a minute or so they would try another sneak attack. With Geronimo and Helen both down, he couldn't afford to wage a running firefight. He couldn't allow the trigger men to harass them. With the realization came action, a maneuver the mobsters would not be expecting. Instead of assisting Geronimo and Helen, instead of helping them to reach the bend, he opted for, as Hickok would say, the direct approach.

He charged the landing.

One of the trigger men was at the slightly open landing door, and he shouted a warning to his fellows as the giant bounded down the steps four at a leap. He poked his shotgun through the opening.

Blade saw the shotgun barrel and fired from the hip, his burst striking the edge of the landing door, splintering and chipping the wood.

There was a gurgling screech from the far side, and the shotgun barrel disappeared.

Blade never missed a beat. He vaulted onto the landing and grabbed the doorknob, flinging the door wide.

The trigger man with the shotgun was on the floor, writhing and convulsing, miniature crimson geysers spouting from his neck and chest, the shotgun lying across his legs.

Three mobsters were left. One, on his knees, was coolly reloading a Marlin. The other two were armed with machine guns, and they automatically swung their weapons toward the doorway as the giant materialized.

Blade fired first.

The pair with machine guns were both stitched across the chest, their bodies propelled backwards to collapse on the hall floor.

Blade pivoted and lowered the Commando barrel to bag the trigger man with the Marlin.

The mobster possessed incredible reflexes. He had dropped the Marlin and sprang toward the giant in a flying tackle as his two associates were mowed down.

Blade never got off a shot. He felt strong arms encircle his legs below the knees and he was knocked backwards, losing his balance and falling, landing hard on his back.

The mobster, a powerful man with dark hair and green eyes, wearing a grey suit, released the giant's legs and lunged, grasping the Commando.

Blade tried to jerk the Commando free, and for several seconds the two men thrashed on the landing, wrestling for control of the gun.

The mobster broke the deadlock by kneeing the giant in the nuts.

A spasm of pain caused Blade to bend forward, his privates twinging, as the man in gray rolled to the left. He saw the mobster's right hand vanish under the gray jacket and reappear holding a 14-inch survival knife. With a monumental effort, his teeth gritting, perspiration beading his forehead, Blade heaved to his feet.

Not expecting the giant to recover so quickly, the mobster had not immediately pressed his advantage. Now he crouched, the survival knife gleaming, his wary eyes on the Commando barrel which was pointing directly at him.

Blade took a deep breath, feeling his privates returning to normal. He noted the look of defiance in the mobster's eyes, and he admired the man's courage.

Several seconds elapsed.

Already perplexed by the giant's hesitation in shooting, the mobster was positively stupefied when the giant unexpectedly placed the Commando on the landing and drew the right Bowie.

"Are you any good with that toothpick of yours?" Blade asked, baiting him.

For an answer, the mobster came in fast and low, swinging the survival knife in a glistening arc.

Blade blocked the blow with a swipe of his Bowie, the two knives clanging as they struck. He backpedaled to avoid another swing, his movements slightly awkward due to lingering discomfort in his groin.

The mobster, noticing, pressed his attack.

Blade parried and evaded a skillful series of feints and jabs. He allowed himself to be forced to the railing, letting the mobster's confidence grow. Overconfidence bred carelessness, an adage proven time and again.

Like now.

Believing he was the superior knifeman, the mobster tried to end the fray quickly by feinting a stab at the giant's stomach, expecting the giant to counter by lowering the Bowie and leaving his neck exposed. So the mobster feinted, then arced his survival knife upward at the giant's throat.

Only the giant wasn't there.

Blade *had* lowered the Bowie to protect his stomach, but he had *also* shifted to the right at the same instant. As the mobster's arm swept the survival knife up, leaving the trigger man's midriff completely unprotected, Blade drove his Bowie into the man's abdomen to the hilt, then twisted.

With a strangled wheeze, the mobster stiffened and started to sag.

His enormous arms bulging, Blade used both hands to slice the Bowie from the mobster's stomach to the sternum. He yanked the Bowie out and stepped aside.

The mobster's eyes were wide and unfocused. His intestines and organs were bulging through the abdominal wound. He tottered forward into the railing and clutched at the top rail for support, but he couldn't seem to get a grip on it. Slowly, so slowly, he limply sagged over the top rail, his arms flailing weakly. With a pathetic whimper he pitched over the railing.

Blade wiped his Bowie on his pants and faced the stairs leading upward. He stopped and retrieved the Commando.

Geronimo was sitting on the step below the bend, the Browning in his lap, his legs drawn inward, staunching the flow of blood from his injured left thigh with a strip of cloth torn from his shirt. He grinned. "It's nice to see you haven't lost your touch."

Blade dashed up the stairs. "Can you walk?"

"I can hobble," Geronimo responded. "But I won't be running any marathons for a while."

"Maybe Helen can . . ." Blade began, then stopped, his eyes narrowing and searching the stairs above. "Where *is* Helen?"

Geronimo jerked his right thumb upward. "She went after Mindy."

"What?"

"She took off for the third floor while you were using that mobster for carving practice," Geronimo explained.

"Damn!" Blade snapped in annoyance. "She's not supposed to make a move without any orders."

"She's a woman, isn't she?" Geronimo remarked.

"What does that have to do with anything?" Blade demanded.

Geronimo chuckled. "How can you be married and ask such a ridiculous question?" he rejoined.

"We've got to go after her," Blade stated. "Here. I'll

give you a hand." He extended his right arm.

"No," Geronimo said. "I'll slow you down. Go on alone. I'll wait here."

"You're coming with me," Blade declared, "and that's final!"

"Fine by me," Geronimo agreed, taking Blade's arm and rising. He stared at his friend for a moment, then grinned. "Has anyone ever told you that your cheeks twitch when you're mad?"

CHAPTER TWENTY

"Don Giorgio!" Ozzi blurted out.

Don Giorgio entered the chamber, Sacks right behind him. The Don carried his Weaver Arms Nighthawk in his left hand. Sacks was armed with a pump shotgun.

Giorgio gazed at Ozzi's face. "What the hell happened to you? You look like you lost a collision with a cement truck."

Ozzi wagged his Bushmaster at the Warrior on the floor. "Hickok," he said simply.

Giorgio frowned as he looked at the Warrior. "Is he dead?"

"No," Ozzi said. "Just unconscious."

"Then we'll finish the son of a bitch off before we leave," the Don stated. He shifted his attention to Mindy. "I want her alive."

"I want to waste her!" Ozzi protested.

"We need her alive," Don Giorgio reiterated. "She's our ticket out of here. Don Pucci's men are in the casino. They'll be here before too long. We're leaving while the leaving is good."

"Where will we go, boss?" Sacks inquired.

"I have hideouts Pucci doesn't know about," Don Giorgio replied. "He hasn't won yet! I'll reorganize and throw everything I have at him."

"Where can Kenney be?" Sacks asked.

"We'll worry about him later," Giorgio said. "Right now, I need to grab my papers from my safe. You two stay put." He walked to a door on the left side of the chamber and went into the next room.

Ozzi glanced at Sacks. "I want the honor of snuffing the Warrior."

Sacks shrugged. "Suit yourself. He means nothing to me."

Mindy gazed from one hit man to the other. "You two are despicable!"

"Listen to who's talking!" Ozzi retorted.

"I hope I'm around when Blade catches up with you," Mindy taunted Ozzi. "I want to see the look on your face."

"Shut up!" Ozzi barked.

Mindy's loathing and resentment supplanted her caution. "Big, tough man, huh?"

"I said shut up!" Ozzi growled.

"We have babies at the Home who are more manly than you'll ever be!" she mocked him.

Ozzi took a step toward her, scowling in fury. "Keep it up, bitch!"

"Ozz!" Sacks said. "The Don needs her alive."

"But he didn't say I couldn't rearrange her face a bit," Ozzi hissed. He jabbed the Bushmaster stock at her face.

Mindy instinctively raised her hands to screen her head.

Which was the reaction Ozzi wanted. He smirked as he rammed the stock into her stomach instead.

Gasping, Mindy doubled over.

Ozzi laughed. "Want some more, scuzz?"

Mindy looked up through tears of anguish. She saw Ozzi cackling, and near the doorway Sacks was staring in disapproval at the younger button man. Sacks started to open his mouth, to say something, but the words never came out.

There was a swishing noise from behind Sacks, and a scintillating, streaking, metallic object swept into the rear of his head.

Sacks arched his back and uttered a choking, inarticulate, panting sound. His eyes bulged, his arms dropping loosely to his sides, the shotgun falling to the floor.

"Sacks?" Ozzi said in surprise.

Sacks took a single step, then keeled over, his head bending downward as he fell, revealing the rear of his cranium; his head was split open from neck to crown.

Mindy straightened in amazement as her gaze alighted on the person responsible for Sacks's demise. "Mom!" she cried.

Helen stood in a martial-arts stance, jodan-no-kamae, her bloody machete held in the same manner as the traditional katana. Her amber hair was disheveled, her black leather vest and pants spattered with gore. Blood caked her right cheek and chin, and her right shoulder was awash in crimson.

"She's your mom?" Ozzi blurted out, and tried to swing the Bushmaster around.

Helen was faster. She closed on the hit man and swung the machete, her blade deflecting the Bushmaster barrel to the right. With the deadly proficiency born of years of practice, she employed a reverse strike, slashing the machete across Ozzi's chest, the keen edge cleaving several inches into his flesh.

Ozzi screamed and frantically tried to back away.

Helen wouldn't let him. She took a measured stride and swung the machete with all her strength, catching the hit man in the throat and nearly decapitating him.

Ozzi was dead on his feet. His head flopped to the left as blood gushed from his ravaged neck, and he sank to the floor in lifeless silence.

Helen glared at the mobster for a second, then moved to Mindy.

"You're hurt!" Mindy exclaimed in alarm.

"It's nothing," Helen said. "A scratch."

For a moment mother and daughter gazed into each other's eyes in mutual love and devotion, and then they embraced in a hug.

"Oh, Mom," Mindy said, sniffling.

"It's over," Helen stated. "You're safe. No one will hurt you now."

"I wouldn't be so sure of that," commented a sarcastic, gruff voice.

Helen spun in the direction of the voice, putting herself between Mindy and the man in black six feet away. She raised the katana.

"I wouldn't, if I were you," the man remarked, pointing his Nighthawk at Helen.

"Don Giorgio!" Mindy declared in stark terror.

"How nice of you to remember me," Giorgio mentioned bitterly. He held the Nighthawk in both hands. On the floor to his right was a brown leather briefcase.

"You're the one who kidnapped Mindy!" Helen stated.

"Give the woman a prize," Don Giorgio taunted her. He looked at Sacks and Ozzi. "You Warriors are more trouble than you're worth."

Helen took a step toward him. "You deserve to die!"

Giorgio's grip on the Nighthawk tightened. "Don't be stupid, woman! You'll be cut to ribbons before you can get within two feet of me."

"You're going to kill us anyway," Helen noted.

Don Giorgio grinned. "True. So which one of you wants it first? Mother or daughter?"

Helen was girding herself for a desperate lunge.

"No answer?" Giorgio scoffed. "Well, then, I'll kill both of you together. What can be more appropriate?"

"How about if you go first, cow chip?" interjected someone in a distinctly familiar Western accent.

Mindy glanced to her right.

Hickok was lying on his stomach on the floor, the Henry snug against his shoulder, sighting down the barrel. He was smiling, his left temple coated with blood.

Don Giorgio froze, the Nighthawk still trained on Helen. He knew Hickok would drill him if he so much as blinked.

"Go ahead," Hickok said. "Make my year!"

Giorgio released the Nighthawk and the gun fell to the carpet. "I'm not an idiot."

"You could have fooled me!" Hickok retorted.

Smiling smugly, Giorgio held his arms up, palms outward. "I know all about you Warriors. You're real spiritual types. You live by some asinine code of honor." He chuckled. "You would never shoot an unarmed man."

"Do you know something?" Hickok asked, raising his chin from the Henry.

"What's that?" Giorgio responded arrogantly.

Hickok's features became an iron mask. "You're wrong."

In a startling flash of insight, Don Johnny Giorgio recognized he was staring death in the face. He took a step backward, fear flooding through him. "No!"

"Yes," Hickok said, and fired.

The heavy slug from the 44-40 lifted Giorgio from his feet and hurled him over a yard to crash onto his back. He pushed himself into a sitting posture and gawked at a gaping hole in the center of his chest. Whining in despair, he stared at the gunfighter.

"Say hello to oblivion for me," Hickok said softly, and squeezed the trigger.

Mindy heard the deafening retort of the Henry even as the top of Don Giorgio's head exploded over the carpet and he was knocked flat. This time Giorgio didn't move.

Hickok slowly stood and walked over to the Don.

"Is he dead?" Mindy queried hopefully.

"They don't come any deader."

EPILOGUE

"Are you positive I can't convince you to stay longer?" Don Pucci asked.

"Thank you for your kindness," Blade responded, "but we've stayed too long as it is. We must return to the Home."

They were standing on the front steps of the Golden Crown Casino. Pedestrians passed on the sidewalk, and the boulevard was filled with traffic.

"Peace has been restored to the city, thanks to you," Don Pucci remarked.

Blade gazed across the boulevard at the Palace. The front entrance was boarded over. "Will you reopen Giorgio's casino?"

"Eventually," Don Pucci said. "I think I'll have Mario run it."

"He's a competent man," Blade remarked.

Loud laughter sounded behind them.

Blade glanced over his right shoulder, smiling at the sight of Hickok, Geronimo, Helen, and Mindy emerging from the Golden Crown. Hickok sported a white bandage on his head, courtesy of the staff at a nearby hospital. Geronimo's right side was bandaged under his shirt, and his left thigh was wrapped tight with a white dressing. He had refused a crutch, and was walking with a pronounced limp. Helen's right cheek had required seven stitches, and her right shoulder was covered by a white binding. Blade reached down and gingerly touched his vest above the area on his right side wounded during the battle. The dressing was itching terribly.

"I tell you, pard!" Hickok declared. "These casinos are great ideas! How about if we try and convince the Elders to build one at the Home?"

"I doubt they'd consent," Blade replied.

"They don't know what they're missing!" Hickok said.

"I know someone who is probably missing you," Blade mentioned. "Your wife. We've been here a week. It's time to hit the road."

Helen walked up to Don Pucci. "Thank you for your hospitality. If you ever get up our way . . ."

"I'll keep the thought in mind," Pucci commented.

"What about the proposal I made?" Blade inquired. "We can always use another member in the Freedom Federation."

"Thanks, but no," Don Pucci said. "We have survived for over a century because we have scrupulously avoided all entanglements. We must uphold our neutrality."

"I understand," Blade commented.

Don Pucci gazed at the giant thoughtfully for several seconds. "There is some information I must pass on to you," he said. "But I must qualify my remarks. As you can imagine, with the thousands and thousands of visitors to Vegas every year, we hear a lot of stories, a lot of rumors. Most of it is worthless hearsay. Exaggerated tales. Inebriated rambling. But we do glean important information from some of our customers. They may mention a fact to a hostess, or to a bartender, or one of the pros. And if the information is considered to be of any merit, it is passed up the chain of command to me." He paused.

"Did you hear something about us?" Hickok asked.

"Was someone blabbin' about Blade's snorin' again?"

Pucci shook his head. "This is most serious. A man passed through Vegas several weeks ago. He spent several nights with one of the pros, and he talked a lot. She didn't think much of it at the time, because the man was a heavy drinker. But everyone in Vegas now knows we are in your debt. And when she realized you are the ones this man was talking about, she came to see me."

"What did this man say?" Blade questioned, his curoisity aroused.

"He told her about this group living in Minnesota," Don Pucci related. "He said his masters—that was the word he used—were planning to eradicate this group known as the Family."

The Warriors exchanged glances.

"Anything else?" Blade probed.

"This man mentioned the name of his masters," Don Pucci divulged. "They are called the Dragons." He frowned. "I have heard of these Dragons, Blade. I don't know a lot about them, but I do know they are based in the former state of Florida. And I know they have a reputation for viciousness unmatched by anyone else."

"Why would these Dragons want to take on the Family?" Hickok interjected. "We've never tangled with them."

"Again," Don Pucci emphasized, "I can't vouch for the reliability of this information. But I thought you should know."

"Thanks," Blade said. "We'll report it to our Leader."

"Is there anything you need before you depart?" Don Pucci inquired.

Blade thought of the SEAL, parked in the lot behind the Golden Crown. Mario had driven him from the city four days before so he could reclaim the transport. "No, thanks. We're fully provisioned and ready to go."

The giant Warrior and the Don shook hands.

"I hope we meet again some day," Don Pucci said.

"Take care," Blade stated. He turned and walked to the sidewalk, bearing to the left, intending to stroll around the

Golden Crown to the rear parking lot.

Hickok, Geronimo, Helen, and Mindy followed him.

"Say, pard," Hickok said, catching up with Blade. "I'd appreciate it if you wouldn't say anything to my missus about me spendin' a week gambling. She might not cotton to the idea."

"I won't lie for you," Blade remarked.

"Who's askin' you to lie?" Hickok queried. "I just don't want to get in trouble."

"You don't need to worry about Blade telling your wife," Geronimo spoke up.

Hickok looked back. "I don't?"

"Nope," Geronimo said, grinning. "Because I will."

"What did I ever do to you?" Hickok demanded.

"Do you want me to list everything?" Geronimo inquired. "There was the time when we were six years old, and you convinced me to take a bath in a mud puddle with my clothes on. Remember that? You claimed everyone did it, and my mother wouldn't mind. She did."

Hickok chuckled. "I'd plumb forgotten all about that."

"And there was the time when we were ten," Geronimo went on. "You persuaded me to stick a frog down Emily's dress. You claimed she loved frogs. She didn't."

Hickok snickered.

"And how about the time when we were fifteen?" Geronimo continued. "We went on a double date, remember? You suggested we should all go skinny-dipping in the moat. We were supposed to each get undressed separately, behind the bushes, then come out and go swimming. But when I stepped out in the open, I was the only one naked."

"I thought the girls would bust a gut laughing," Hickok recalled, and laughed.

"And you have the gall to ask about my reason for telling your wife?" Geronimo asked in amazement.

Hickok sighed and glanced at Blade. "It's pitiful."

"What is?" Blade responded.

"This mangy Injun is one of my best friends," Hickok muttered.

"I know. So?" Blade said.

"So with friends like him, is it any wonder I'm always in hot water?" Hickok lamented his fate.

Blade smiled. "Look at it from our perspective."

"What do you mean?" Hickok inquired.

"With a friend like you around," Blade said, "there's never a dull moment."

AFTER THE NUCLEAR WAR WAS OVER — THE REAL KILLING BEGAN

They called him Phoenix because he rose from the ashes of destruction, driven by hatred, and thirsting for revenge. Battling nature gone insane and men driven mad by total devastation, he forged his way across a nightmare landscape.

The action/adventure series that's hotter than a thermonuclear explosion, by

DAVID ALEXANDER

_____2462-4   #1:   DARK MESSIAH
$2.95 US/$3.75 CAN

_____2517-5   #2:   GROUND ZERO
$2.95 US/$3.75 CAN

_____2571-X   #3:   DEATH QUEST
$2.95US/$3.75 CAN

LEISURE BOOKS
ATTN: Customer Service Dept.
276 5th Avenue. New York, NY 10001

Please send me the book(s) checked above. I have enclosed $_____
Add $1.25 for shipping and handling for the first book; $ .30 for each book thereafter. No cash. stamps. or C.O.D.s. All orders shipped within 6 weeks. Canadian orders please add $1.00 extra postage.

Name _____

Address _____

City_____State_____Zip_____

Canadian orders must be paid in U.S. dollars payable through a New York banking facility.   ☐ Please send a free catalogue.